SATED

REBEKAH
WEATHERSPOON

BOOKS BY REBEKAH

STAND ALONE TITLES
The Fling
At Her Feet
Treasure

VAMPIRE SORORITY SISTERS
Better Off Red
Blacker Than Blue
Soul To Keep

THE FIT TRILOGY
Fit
Tamed
Sated

SUGAR BABY NOVELLAS
So Sweet
So Right
So For Real

PRAISE FOR FIT (#1 IN THE FIT TRILOGY)

"I felt satisfied by a complete story at the end, and would highly recommend this to anyone looking for a fun, relatable contemporary romance."
- Elisa Verna, *Romantic Times Book Reviews*
(TOP PICK REVIEW)

"This is a delightful, sexy short romance that made me eager to read the next one!"
- Rachel Kramer Bussel,
HeroesandHeartbreakers.com

PRAISE FOR TAMED

"The second in Weatherspoon's Fit series, 'Tamed' is another must-read for fans of BDSM romance.
- Elisa Verna, *Romantic Times Book Reviews*
(TOP PICK REVIEW)

DEDICATION

To Fangirls Everywhere!

ACKNOWLEDGEMENTS

Anya Richards

KB Alan

Beverly Diehl

Tecora Arnold

Solace Ames

Minx Malone

And everyone who waited patiently for the final installment

Thank you.

CHAPTER ONE

Keira took the dessert menu even though she was full. She was determined to save this date.

"Everything looks good," she said, trying to sound cheerful. She glanced up at the man sitting across from her. Travis Humphrey, power forward for the LA Clippers. He was good-looking, on TV at least, but from the moment he'd met her outside the restaurant he became more and more unattractive with every word he spoke. He wasn't speaking anymore though. He was looking at his phone.

Why do I keep doing this to myself? Keira thought. *Oh, you know why.*

She did. She'd been single for almost two years and completely sex free for almost ten months. Being a massive dork, who enjoyed spending the majority of her time on fan-based blogs or in a movie theater alone, didn't make the quest for a life mate any easier. And this nagging need to find a man seemed that much worse when Keira stepped back and looked at how great her life was. She had plenty to be thankful for. A great job teaching kickboxing and doing a little personal training at Melrose Fitness, one of the best gyms in town. She had amazing parents who doted on her, and plenty of great friends. Keira had it all, except a date who could give her his undivided attention through an entire meal.

Before the evening even kicked off, all signs pointed to disaster. Keira picked out the perfect dress. Her cousin was sweet enough to come over and do her hair. Even the weather was just right. The day had been unusually hot for November, but by the time she'd stepped out of her North Hollywood apartment, things had cooled off to a perfect degree. Everything was in place as she drove to meet Travis at Más. Everything was too right. She was putting in too much effort for a guy she didn't even like. That's how desperate her situation had become.

The fact that Travis hadn't been the one to ask her out and she still said yes? That should have been the first red flag. His assistant did the legwork. Travis had seen her across the room at a charity function and sent the young kid over with his cell phone out and ready to receive some digits. Travis flashed her a smile when his assistant pointed him out to Keira.

It wasn't charming in the slightest, but when was the last time someone had asked her on a date without yelling the words "Eh girl!" from across the street or sending a message on DotComCupid asking for nudes? She said sure and gave the assistant her number. Travis was courteous enough to call himself, but the conversation was short and filled with innuendo. He had one thing in mind. Keira wasn't sure she was going to give that one thing up, not on the first date. She wanted to see if there was any real chemistry between them.

There wasn't.

"You wanna split something?" Keira tried again.

"Nah, I'm not much on sweet. But I got you. Get whatever you want." He glanced up from his phone, finally, and flashed her that smile that must work wonders on other women. Who was she kidding? The smile had worked on her.

Keira put the menu down. It was time to wrap up this waste of an evening. "I think I'll pass too. You have plans for this weekend?"

"Flying down to Miami with my boys. Playing the Heat. But after the game we're always looking for more company."

"Oh," Keira tried to sound disappointed. "Thanks for the invitation, but I can't."

Travis leaned forward. He'd been doing that all night, arching an eyebrow and testing the support strength of the table legs. She was only two feet away. She could hear him just fine. But that didn't matter.

He had to get closer and take any chance he got to turn the conversation toward sex. That's when he was all interest, completely engaged, and probably at full attention. "What'd you have going on that's better than hitting South Beach?"

"I…" Keira had a day pass to Galaxi-Con, the annual convention for only her favorite show in the whole freaking universe. She'd already told her boss-buddies, Grant and Armando, they were going to have to cover her schedule at the gym. She had her cosplay outfit planned with two back-ups just in case the she wasn't up to full body makeup for a whole day. She almost told Travis about it, but something about the way he was glancing at his phone again, kind of waiting for her answer, mostly waiting to get her in the sack, made Keira think he wouldn't be interested.

Screw it, Keira thought. *Tell him.*

"I actually have tickets to Galaxi-Con. Do you watch *Galaxis*?"

"Nah. What is it?"

Oh, he really screwed up. Geek-mode, activated. "It's this really cool show. It's basically about this girl, well this young woman, Orora. She's living on this Earth-like colony on the outskirts of the galaxy. Part human, part alien and totally orphaned, she finds out that she's actually the heir to this whole kingdom and she has to get back to Earth and stop the remaining humans from killing her mother's people."

Travis completely checked out, looking from his phone to his watch, to the women at the table just to Keira's left, but Keira kept talking, five seasons worth of nerdiness. She even dropped some bits about the fanfiction she'd been writing and how many friends she'd made online because of it. Travis could not be less interested.

Their server came back, all smiles. "Did we decide? Any dessert?"

Keira tried to smile back. "No, thank—"

"Nah, we're good." Keira could feel herself frowning as Travis reached into his wallet then threw a bunch of cash on the table before he moved to stand up. It was more than enough to cover the bill, but geez. Manners much?

"Ready?" he asked.

"Uh, yeah." Keira offered a quiet apology to their server then followed Travis out of the restaurant. As soon as they hit the door, she cut right for the valet stand. The street was swarming with paparazzi, but Travis didn't seem to mind.

"Yo, Travis! Yo, Travis! You on a date, man?"

"Nah, just out with some friends."

Keira felt the hot light from a camera turn toward her. She almost jumped behind a potted plant, but thought better of it. She raised her clutch instead and covered her face.

"Leave her alone, man. We're just friends."

"You sure, bro?"

"Positive."

Keira listened on as the pap started asking Travis about his watch and how he saw the rest of the season going. He sounded happier than he'd been all night. Good to know they'd *both* had a terrible time. Eventually he got tired of the lights and cameras and came over to join her. The valet attendant already had his car waiting.

"So you wanna come back to my place?" he asked, just as her car pulled up.

She walked around to the driver's side, putting her Dodge Challenger between them. He had no interest in anything she had to say, but she had a feeling he might go in for the kiss. A final attempt at persuasion.

"I'd love to, but I have a client early in the morning." Both lies rolled easily off her tongue.

"What do you do again?"

Keira glared at him for a moment. She'd told him about Melrose Fitness, at length. In the brief moment when he'd actually been paying attention, he'd teased her, in his not so charming way, about her kickboxing skills and how he was sure he could still take her.

"I'm a vet tech. Pit bull puppies first thing in the morning. Have to be alert to deal with that handful."

"Oh aight. Cool—"

Keira didn't wait for him to finish his sentence. She tipped the valet, then slid into her car. Before she turned the corner onto the next street, she caught a glimpse of Travis in her rear view mirror. Three women heading into the restaurant already had his attention. Keira made up her mind right then and there, she was never dating again.

The gym was quiet except for the sound of Keira's foot striking the bag. She was exhausted. Sweat poured down her face and her hip was starting to ache, but her feelings for Travis Humphrey were almost all worked out. Well, more like her non-feelings for Travis Humphrey. And that's what pissed her off so much. How could she be so upset over a guy that was clearly wrong for her? You could see how poorly matched they were from outer space. Still she couldn't help feeling as if she'd failed again; failed to live up to some weird standards she'd created for herself. Like she'd failed to be enough.

Her mother had always told her that her looks would only get her so far. From the time she could comprehend compliments, people had always told her how beautiful she was, but Keira took her mother's words directly to heart and made it her life's goal to not only develop her physical but her mental strength. When she wasn't in the gym, her face was buried in a book or a comic, or focused on the nearest screen playing her sci-fi favorites. Keira had crafted herself into the dream student, the model child, and the ideal athlete. And the most socially awkward human being ever.

No one cared about her favorite books and TV shows, no one except her friends online. And only Grant and Armando gave a crap about how many hand-stand push ups she could do. She got along great with Armando. He treated her like a little sister; a little sister he sort of put up with. She wasn't super close with Grant, even though he'd been the one to hire her. They were both super nice, but they were also her bosses, and they saw what she could bring to their gym as a female fitness instructor.

At the moment, both of them were gone. Armando was returning from a trip at some point that day and Grant had stepped out to join his girlfriend, Violet, for lunch. Keira had the gym to herself until he came back and the afternoon sessions with clients kicked up again. Keira knew she should chill out and mentally prepare to spend the rest of the day smiling at people, but she could not shake this funk. She worked her fists, punching the crap out of the bag for a few more minutes. Then Armando came bounding through the gym's frosted double doors.

"Well hello, Keira," he said cheerfully, as he walked by. "See the place didn't blow up while I was gone."

"Yeah, we managed," Keira mumbled. Armando popped into the back office. He reappeared a minute later, chest bare, carrying a Melrose Fitness shirt in his hand. Keira tried not to look. He was taken too, but a nice body was a nice body.

"What's going on?" he asked.

"Nothing." Keira delivered another hard kick. More sweat slicked down her back.

"You okay?"

"Peachy."

"Hey. What's going on?" Armando grabbed the bag and held it in place. That didn't stop Keira from throwing a few more punches. She glanced up at his face. He wasn't going to leave her alone until she talked. Keira sank to the floor and started pulling off her wraps.

"I went out with Travis Humphrey last night and it was terrible."

"What happened? Did he try any funny business?"

That made Keira laugh. "He hinted heavily at the funny business, but he didn't try anything. I just don't know why I bother. I go on so many first dates, but guys never seem to like me. Maybe I'm just too buff. Some guys don't do muscles." She playfully poked at her sweaty bicep.

"That's not it. You're too pretty."

She looked up at Armando, scowling. "Thanks?"

"Listen. Men are functional morons. We take everything at face value. We see a hot woman and we think about sex and nothing else until we actually speak to you. And then some of us, the assholes mainly, can't believe it when a woman comes with weird shit like a brain and her own personality. Look, it's stupid, but we have a hard time seeing past a pretty face sometimes. Shit, even I read you all wrong when we first met."

"You did?"

"Yeah, ask Grant. I was pissed when he hired you. I had to force myself not to ask you out."

"Cause you're my boss?"

"Pretty much. But then I got to know you and I realized—"

"You realized that we're such good friends. That I remind you of your little sister. I know, I know. Connie and I are practically personality twins."

"You are, but that's not it. I realized that we'd be terrible together."

Keira flopped onto her back. "You're not helping."

"Come on. You know I love you to death, but could you honestly see us together?"

"No." And it wasn't because he was her boss. Armando and Grant were both funny, sweet guys, but something about them always made Keira feel like they were on a different level of cool adultness. Didn't help that both of them were involved in some bondage club, freaky domination type stuff. It intrigued her, but she could never be on the receiving end of that kind of torture and, from what she's witnessed between Armando and his girlfriend, he was only into giving.

"Dude, you've met Nailah. You see how much I love her. Or look at Grant and Violet. He's a teddy bear and she's Miss Skeptical-Sarcasm."

Armando had a point. Nailah had a very cool demeanor that you had to chip away at. Once you got to know her though, she was sweet as pie. They weren't friends, exactly, but Keira liked Nailah a lot and seeing her with Armando, it was clear how good they were together. He was hot and she was cold. Keira herself was also hot, cheerful and outgoing, just like Armando and Grant. Their upbeat personalities made it so easy for them to get along, made it easy for the three of them to run the gym so smoothly, but there was nothing romantic there. It wouldn't make sense. Dating Grant or Armando would be like dating herself.

"Seems like opposites do attract, but it's not like Travis and I were too much alike."

"Something tells me that you and a guy like Travis Humphrey have nothing to connect on at all."

"And I don't even like him! Ugh, you're right, but what am I going to do? It's not like…" Keira let out a deep breath. "I know I don't *need* a man—"

"Keira, stop." Armando's tone was too serious. The sound of it made her look up again. "You need what you need and if you need someone in your life who cares about you that way, then there's nothing wrong with that. Just don't rush it. If you want the real thing, be patient. He'll come along."

"When did you get so insightful?"

"Blame Nailah. She makes me think about crap like feelings and shit."

"I'll have to thank her."

"You're going to that comic thing this weekend and you said your Internet buddies bailed, right?" It wasn't some comic thing, but Keira was too tired to correct him.

"Yeah."

"You should meet up with my buddy, Daniel. His brother is involved with the show. I'm sure he can hook you up with some behind-the-scenes perks. Help you take your mind off this dating crap."

Keira remembered meeting Daniel once and she only remembered because he was an intensely hot Asian guy who'd had one of his hands amputated. He also had a really deep voice that threw her off a bit. They hadn't said more than a hello to each other at Grant's last birthday party, but he was hard to forget.

"It would be nice not to walk around the convention alone." She had planned to meet up with a few friends from the *Galaxis* blogs but, for one reason or another, each of them was unable to make the trip to Los Angeles this year.

"Cool. I'll text him. I'm sure he has some sort of VIP access. You'll have fun."

Grant walked in then, face a little flushed, grinning from ear to ear. Lunch with Violet probably hadn't involved any food.

"Hey! What are we doing?" he asked, as he lightly slapped the heavy bag still hanging near Armando's head.

"I was just telling Keira she should go to the that Con thing with Daniel. You know, let him show her around."

"Daniel Song?"

"Yep."

Grant's hesitation made Keira's stomach sink. They couldn't even find people who wanted to spend an afternoon with her. "Bad idea?"

"No, no. Not at all," Grant said, cocking his head to the side. "I just realized you guys have never hung out. He's a cool guy. And I think his brother is big in the sci-fi TV world. You should have a good time with him."

"See? Forget about dating for a while. Just go to the comic con and have some fun." Armando patted Keira on the leg before he stood up and pulled on his shirt. Keira hoped this was a good idea. If not, she was fully prepared to ditch Daniel. She could geek out on her own.

✶

Daniel stood in the middle of the arena floor, eying the stage. He hated last-minute jobs, but it kind of went against company policy at Fire In The Sky Pyrotechnics to leave a new client in the lurch.

Forty-eight hours prior, as his first nationwide tour kicked off in San Diego, "teen sensation" Blake Carlisle had to end the show when not one, but two of his pyro effects malfunctioned. The first caught the pants of a backup dancer on fire, but roadies were able to stop, drop, and roll her before any bodily damage was done. She was back for the next number, in new pants.

The fans to the left of the stage weren't so lucky when a flame tower tumbled into the audience. Two dozen concertgoers were sent to the ER with severe burns and other injuries. Blake's tour management had immediately fired the previous pyro team and stuck them with the legal problems, but the show had to go on. Daniel had a day to figure out how to fix or replace the stunts before the tour took up again at the Staples Center. He'd wished he'd brought earplugs though. They were doing a run-through of the whole show so Daniel could fix the issues, but the kid's music sucked.

"The stage is too small," Daniel said to his partner, Mike. Daniel gestured to the right side of the stage with his prosthesis. Sometimes it caused some discomfort, but he always wore it to work. Helped him manipulate the charges better and it scared newbies who thought you could fuck around with fire and not get burned. The body-powered beauty was black with a black hook attachment. He did like that it got people's attention. "And they based the tower right on that slope. I'm surprised it didn't take out more people."

"Should we kill the fire all together?" Mike asked.

"That's what I'm thinking." Daniel looked down, as his phone vibrated in his palm. He expected his mother, checking in after her shift at the casino, but the number of a good friend of his, a buddy-in-kink, Armando Vasquez, lit up the screen instead. He'd known Armando and his business partner Grant for years. Daniel had taught them both a thing or two about wielding a flog. And dealing with male submissives. He usually caught up with them a few times a month at the bondage club Daniel's close confidants and mentors owned. Master Philip's or "The Club" as it was also known, was where all three of them had come into their own as masters of their sexual needs and desires. He'd spent some of the best nights of his life in that refurbished warehouse, recovering, playing, growing as the man and switch he wanted to be. There was nothing on The Club calendar that coming weekend, but maybe Armando had something else in mind.

Blake was still mid-performance, but Daniel answered anyway. He had the gist of this shit-show.

"Vasquez, what's going on?" Daniel asked over the music.

"Not much. You busy?"

"Sort of. Just a last minute consult. What's up?"

"Question for you. You're still going to that convention this weekend, right?"

"Galaxi-Con? Yeah. Why? What's up?"

"You feel like some company?"

"You want to go?" Armando was cool and all, but conventions for popular sci-fi shows didn't seem like his thing. Fan conventions weren't really Daniel's thing either, but he'd promised his mom he would show up and support his brother.

"No, I had someone else in mind. I think you might know her."

Daniel listened as Armando laid out the particulars for what sounded like an adult play date with his co-worker, Keira. Daniel had only met her once, but she seemed like a nice girl and smoking fine, if his memory served him correctly. Armando was quick to explain that she was just looking for someone to hang out with while she took in the day's events. Apparently Keira was a hardcore fan of *Galaxis*, but none of her local friends shared her enthusiasm.

"Yeah, send me her number and I'll call her. I'll make sure she has a good time."

"Thanks, man. I appreciate it, but, uh, one more thing."

"What's that?"

"She's…not like us."

"What? A dude?"

"No, dick. She's vanilla. Very vanilla. She knows about Grant and I, but it totally weirds her out, so don't—"

"So don't ask her back to my place to make a spanking video. Don't worry. I'll keep the kink talk to myself."

"Thanks. I owe you one."

Daniel ended the call and turned his full attention back to the train wreck falsely labeled as entertainment playing out on the stage before him.

CHAPTER TWO

Keira waited by the front doors of the LAX Westin. She'd decided against her Naymorian villager costume, which called for head-to-toe purple body paint, but only took one dedicated step down and dressed as Princess Orora from episode 1.16, "The Coronation". It took forever and some serious online searching, and maybe a YouTube tutorial or two, or five, but Keira managed to fashion Orora's teal gown and jeweled tiara. The makeup was simple enough, just a series of silver dots placed across her face, over the bridge of her nose. The gown though was a showstopper, as was evident by the number of people who had already stopped to take pictures with her in the few short minutes she'd been waiting for her con-companion for the day.

When she agreed to meet with Daniel, the conversation had been kind of quick. They were both busy with work and ended up ironing out the details over text. She wasn't sure what to expect when he showed up, but she just hoped he was ready to dive right in to all the *Galaxis* related fun. A nerd through and through, she was going to gush over the actors during the afternoon panel. She was going to get in line and ask some questions. She was going to partake in the trivia games, and she was going to take pictures, and buy a t-shirt, hopefully some original art, and the only Orora figurines she was missing from her collection. And she was going to be as happy as a pig in poop doing it all. Hopefully Daniel could keep up.

"Keira?"

She swung around at the sound of a deep voice. There was Daniel, just stepping through the hotel doors. Keira blinked. She'd remembered that Daniel was attractive—Grant and Armando were allergic to having ugly friends—but she hadn't remembered him being quite so good-looking. And she'd forgotten just how resonant his voice was. She could feel it under her skin.

Keira watched him as he came closer, all six-plus feet of him. He was dressed plainly, in a white t-shirt, black jeans and black boots, but his clothes fit him so well. You could see the muscle definition through his shirt. He wore his hair kind of like Armando did, shaved on the sides and along the back, but thick black waves on top were styled in a 50's kind of way, with just a touch of hipster. It worked for him.

"It's nice to see you again," he said, reaching out with his left hand to greet her properly. Too busy staring at his face, Keira stuck out her right hand, which resulted in one of those awkward upside-down handshakes.

"Oh, sorry." She laughed nervously.

"It's okay." He smiled back.

"I didn't see you drive up."

"I got here earlier. Didn't know what the parking situation would be like."

"Understandable. I made sure I bought parking vouchers with my convention pass."

"Smart." He took a step back and looked her up and down. "I thought about dressing up, but I'm glad I didn't."

"Why?"

"I don't want to take focus off you. Armando told me you were going all out."

Just then a mother and her young daughter walked over. The little girl was also dressed in Princess Orora's coronation gown.

"Hi, sorry," the woman said. "Can we take a picture with you? You're the first cosplayer she's seen today."

"Of course!"

Keira posed for a few pictures with the little girl, then Daniel snapped a few so the mom could hop in the photos as well. When they were alone again, Keira glanced up to find Daniel staring at her with his striking brown eyes. She felt her face heat up.

"What?"

"Nothing," he said with a hint of a smile. "After you."

Keira ducked her head to hide her embarrassment. She wasn't used to guys looking at her like they were actually looking at her. That subtle smile still in place, Daniel guided her through the hotel doors with his hand gently touching her back, touching the skin exposed by the cut-outs in her Naymorian gown. She did her best to ignore the goose bumps that popped up all over her body.

Keira couldn't believe how much fun she was having. She couldn't believe how much fun she was having *with* Daniel. He stuck by her the whole day, as she bounced from vendor to vendor and panel to panel. He held the stuff she accumulated while she posed for dozens of pictures. He encouraged her to enter the costume contest being held before the main panel of the day. She didn't win, but she won an honorable mention prize, a replica of the pins the Galaxis fighters wore on their uniforms.

The highlight of her day came when it was time to head to the grand ballroom. The line was ridiculously long. Keira was afraid she wouldn't get in, let alone get near one of the mics for the Q&A, but that didn't matter. Daniel had an in. Turns out his brother's "involvement" in the show really meant that his brother was JD Song, who played Orora's love interest on *Galaxis*. A few words to the guys at the door got them to the front of the line and back to the green room after the Q&A.

It wasn't like she should have made the connection. It wasn't like everyone with the last name Song was related. Plus JD spent his whole run on the show in full Naymorian make-up, complete with a flattened nose and massively enlarged eyes. Also, he and Daniel didn't really look alike.

Still, it was great to meet him. JD introduced her to the rest of the cast, including Selia Monroe, the actress who played Princess Orora. She went on about Keira's costume and somehow Keira managed not to break down in crazed fangirly tears. There was a Naymorian ball that was meant to wrap up the day's events, but neither Keira or Daniel were in the mood to dance, so Daniel suggested they continue their evening at a diner up the street.

"I wish Armando had told me about your brother. I wouldn't have dragged you around with me all day. You could have spent time with him," Keira said, as they settled into the tiny booth. She felt bad for monopolizing Daniel's time, but she could not stop smiling.

"No, it's fine. We hung out last night and this morning."

"But you had to listen to me all day. Sorry I'm such a dork about the show."

Daniel shook his head at Keira's bashful smile. "Trust me, I enjoyed it. It's nice to meet someone so passionate about something my brother works on."

"You mean disturbingly obsessed?"

Daniel laughed and picked up his menu. "Maybe a little."

"I thought I was going to cry when he introduced me to Selia."

"I'm sure she's used to it. It's a popular show."

"It is."

Still smiling, Keira watched Daniel for a moment as he looked over their dinner options. He really was good-looking. And he was sweet, kind of soft-spoken—as soft-spoken as anyone could be with a voice like that—and witty. He only had nice things to say all day, even though Keira could tell he was having about an eighth of the fun she was. She liked him a lot so far, but she wanted to like him more. Which was good, right? Armando hadn't meant to "set them up" so to speak, but if the shoe looked like it worth trying on...

Keira squeezed her eyes closed and almost hid under the table. She'd really just compared Daniel to a shoe. At least she hadn't said the stupid words out loud. Just a quick second to clear her throat and she gave not sounding like a complete dummy a shot.

"We spent the whole day focused on me and my *Galaxis* problem. Tell me about you. What do you do? Armando never told me."

"Thank you for asking. I'm part owner of Fire in the Sky Pyrotechnics. Spend most of my time designing fireworks and fire displays."

"That's so cool. I was going ask you what you do in your free time, but—"

"But, what?"

"Actually, I'm sorry. I was about to say something super rude." See, this was the real reason Keira was single, her inappropriate verbal diarrhea. She did not know when to keep her mouth shut and that just plain turned guys off. Maybe if she buried her face in the menu Daniel would forget she was there.

No such luck. He nudged her foot under the table. "I can handle it. Tell me."

"Oh, geez. Okay. I was going to ask what you do in your free time, but I know you hang out with Armando and Grant. And I know what they do in their free time."

"Did they tell you all about it?"

"No…I just…know. They aren't rubbing anything in my face, but they aren't exactly hush-hush about it either. And Armando posts things on Facebook sometimes."

"And what do you think about it?"

Keira shrugged. "I don't really know."

"Do you know much about sadomasochistic practices and power exchange?"

Keira's mind blanked for a second. She had no idea what he was talking about, but she wasn't about to admit that. "I just know they like control or whatever. They like bossing Violet and Nailah around, telling them what to do. And then there's lots of sex involved. It's not really my thing."

That small smile touched the corner of his lips again. Keira wanted to be annoyed with him but she couldn't. And then she realized what she'd said.

"No! I like sex! I definitely like sex—"

"It's more than that, but I see what you're saying. It's not for everyone."

"I'll be honest. Most of what I know it, I learned from fanfiction."

Daniel's eyebrows shot up. "Really?"

He shouldn't have said that. Keira felt her geek mode activating again. "There's this AU fic where Orora— Are you sure you want to hear this?"

"After you tell me what the hell an AU fic is, yes I do."

"It means Alternate Universe. So Orora is a florist and she lives next door to JD's character, and he's a carpenter and he seduces her and ties her up and—"

"Okay, stop. I don't want to think about my brother seducing anyone or what follows."

"Right. Sorry."

"You liked the story though?"

"Yeah. I like reading it, but the stuff he made her do? Not my thing."

"Why's that? Not that I'm trying to persuade you."

"I don't like being told what to do, even if sex comes as a perk."

"I gotcha." Daniel let the subject drop and turned his attention to the menu, but then Keira's curiosity was piqued.

"What's the draw for you, if you don't mind me asking?"

"I don't mind, I just don't want to make you uncomfortable."

"I'm good. One hundred percent comfortable. Go."

"Alright. How can I put this? I may roll with Grant and Armando, but we're into different aspects of the lifestyle. They are Dominants, clear and easy. I'm what you would call a switch."

"I don't know what that is," Keira said.

"I like to play both sides. I can do what your boys do. Have a partner or partners who agree to follow my lead. I can act as Master and Dominant, give out the orders, take the control. And just as easily I can submit."

Keira swallowed as she felt her face heating up. She did not mean for the conversation to go anywhere near this direction, but now she was interested. And possibly picturing Daniel doing all sorts of things with his shirt off. "Which do you like more?"

"I'm most at peace when I'm submitting. What looks good to you?"

"Oh, ah. I think I'm going to get the waffles. I'm sorry. We don't have to talk about this. What are you going to get?"

"The waffles actually sound pretty good. We can talk about whatever you like. Armando mentioned to me that you weren't into kink. *You* just told me you weren't into kink, but I'll go on if you want to know more?"

"He wasn't wrong, but will I sound like a complete hypocrite if I say yes, I do want to know more? Armando and Grant are more like brothers. I can't really talk to them about sex."

"Nothing hypocritical about being curious. But before I get into it, let me tell you about some of my other interests."

"Oh yes. Please do."

"I enjoy puzzles and I love to bowl. And I try to go to the movies at least once a week."

"No, wait. Let's go back to the puzzles."

"I love puzzles." Daniel lifted his arm off the table a bit. "They helped me with my rehab and they've been a bit more of hobby ever since."

"Interesting. Do you mind me asking how…? Jesus. Never mind." Keira really, *really* needed to shut up, but Daniel just laughed her latest faux pass off.

"It was an accident on my first set. Our lead was an idiot, didn't check to see if I was clear of the blast zone and the effects went off."

"Oh my god."

"I'm on the mend, I promise you." That wink of his was too much.

"I see that. Um, back to your other interests. You said something about going to the movies. Would you…like to go with me some time?" Keira took the leap then instantly regretted it when Daniel practically froze behind his menu. "Sorry. I know this wasn't that kind of hang out. I just—"

"No. I would love to."

"Are you sure? You're not saying yes now to be nice, but then you're gonna call me sometime next week and tell me you can't?"

"No, no. How about this? Keira, would you like to go on date with me in the next seven days. Your schedule permitting, of course?"

"I would love that."

"Excellent. Now I say we see about these waffles and then I'll tell you more about my attempt at the jigsaw puzzle world record and how I was off by a full fifteen minutes."

Keira managed to hold back her laughter, but still she smiled.

✱

Keira plopped down on her couch with her laptop. As soon as she pulled it open, a chat box lit up the screen.

LoriNLynn+Twins: TELL ME EVERYTHING!!!

Keira snorted at her friend's enthusiasm. Lori was one of several online buddies who had to back out of the Con, and the person Keira missed the most. She lived in Milwaukee with her wife and their kids. Unfortunately wife and the kids came down with a horrible flu and Lori couldn't bear to leave them. Keira understood, but she was still bummed. Lori was her best fandom friend. They'd only met in person once, but they talked on the phone or online and texted every day.

ItsKeiraTime: How are the babies?

LoriNLynn+Twins: there is snot everywhere. i have kid snot in my fucking hair. and Sammy threw up on me this afternoon.

ItsKeiraTime: lol omg im so sorry.

LoriNLynn+Twins: tell me your day was better than mine. how was the con? send me all the pics. did you get to see Selia? was JD there? Did JD take off his shirt? did Selia take off her shirt? did they simulate a sex act on stage during the panel?

This was why Keira loved Lori; she was just as obsessed with everything *Galaxis* as Keira was.

ItsKeiraTime: no sex, but i think i got a date out of it.

LoriNLynn+Twins: what? SPILL!!!

Keira set about explaining how she met up with Daniel at the convention and how she'd ended up asking him out, even though their time together was only supposed to be a friend-type thing. Then she casually mentioned that Daniel was JD's brother.

LoriNLynn+Twins: WHAT THE FUCK!!! I feel awful for abandoning you and then you end up scoring a date with JD's brother??

ItsKeiraTime: i know. he introduced me to JD and Selia too.

LoriNLynn+Twins: Brb dying on the floor. i can't fucking believe this. should I ditch you more often?

ItsKeiraTime: maybe.

LoriNLynn+Twins: why don't you sound more psyched? you met JD and Selia and now you have a chance to pork JD's brother. I can feel it through the computer. you're not psyched.

Keira knew exactly what was bothering her. She'd had such a good time with Daniel, and he was so cute, but...

ItsKeiraTime: I think I might have spoke too soon. Jumped the gun in asking him out. He's into the bondage stuff.

She included a somewhat conflicted frowny face.

LoriNLynn+Twins: And?? Let him tie you up.

ItsKeiraTime: No!

ItsKeiraTime: He's the real deal, Lor.

Not that she actually knew for sure, but from the way he talked and the mere fact that he ran in the same circles as Grant and Armando? Yeah, they were pros. And Keira? She wasn't, nor did she want to be, any type of sexual professional.

LoriNLynn+Twins: What made you say yes, then? Did we not learn a lesson with Travis McLoser? Don't go out with guys you don't like.

ItsKeiraTime: I DO like him. That's the problem.

LoriNLynn+Twins: Afraid you'll let him do more than tie you up?

That was exactly what Keira was afraid of. What if she ended up really crushing on Daniel? What if he ended up being really good in bed and he turned her into some weirdo perverted sex addict who had to go to therapy because she'd been arrested for public indecency?

Keira's mind continued to run wild. Too many what-ifs. She wanted a boyfriend, but she wasn't so sure she wanted a boyfriend who was a freak.

ItsKeiraTime: He said he's a switch.

LoriNLynn+Twins: Oooh that means he goes both ways! You can tie him up.

ItsKeiraTime: How do you know all this?

LoriNLynn+Twins: google, honey. the internet is your friend. just do it. go out with him once. for me. i need this excitement.

ItsKeiraTime: aren't you gay?

LoriNLynn+Twin: kid. snot. in. my. hair. i need this excitement.

Keira leaned back against her couch, her laugh turning into a sigh. She wasn't going to back out of her date with Daniel, but she needed something. Some sort of reassurance that everything was going to be okay. She had to know more about Daniel. She had to know he could seriously be with someone like Keira, someone who wasn't into those kinky things. She had to talk to Armando and Grant.

Two days later and Daniel's head was still all fucked up, clouded with different flavors of regret. He regretted not kissing Keira before they parted ways the night of the convention. He'd known a lot of people, fucked a lot of people, but as corny as the thought seemed, he'd never met anyone like Keira. Genuine was the best way to describe her; or maybe honest.

He was proud of JD and the career he'd made for himself. Hollywood was not an easy place for Korean actors to navigate, but his brother was doing it. *Galaxis* was his brother's livelihood and further proof that their mother had been right, encouraging them both to chase their dreams. But Daniel had only watched the show to support JD. He'd known fans of the material, but he'd never encountered a fan like Keira. He found her enthusiasm for the whole culture of the fictional world to be insanely attractive. He liked that she wasn't too shy to embrace her inner nerd in front of strangers. He loved that he got to see the real her the first time they met.

He got the feeling Keira wasn't one to hide any part of herself and he dug that. Problem was, she wasn't into kink, and that right there made him regret the hell out of taking her up on her invitation to spend more time together. Kink wasn't just something he was into in his free time, as Keira had suggested. Kink was his life.

He'd been into sadomasochism in some capacity since he was a kid. Along with setting things on fire, he started messing with bondage and pain play around the age of nine. Luckily his mom didn't discourage either. Scouts, and apprenticeships with some of the stage acts at the Bellagio had handled most of his curiosity, helped him perfect his knots, but it wasn't until he found Mistress Evelyn that he'd come to understand exactly what was going on in his head. He really only played with or even dated people he'd met through her and her husband, Master Philip.

He'd become so accustomed to his life as a switch, so comfortable with other members of the community, that spending a romantic evening without some element of BD or SM didn't make a bit of sense. So why was he even considering seeing this girl again? Why had he asked her out?

Various reasons ran through his head. She's beautiful. She's smart. She blurts out exactly what's she's thinking and it's adorable as hell. Even with her dark brown skin, he could tell when she was blushing. He wanted to see that smile again. He wanted to see if he could push her buttons, in a good way. He wanted something different.

He'd drawn up a solution for Blake Carlisle's stage show, then sent a team out to finish the tour. He'd gotten word that things were going smoothly, but he couldn't think too much on it. He had other, more important projects coming down the line.

Yeah, he definitely should have kissed her, but something told him he should wait. He wanted her to make the first move or least tell him when she was ready for him to call the shots. She'd told him that he'd hear from her via text, her preferred mode of communication, but she hadn't reached out to him yet. He hoped she wasn't following that stupid three-day rule. He supposed he could text her first…

Daniel rolled his neck and clicked back into his email. The subject lines started to blur together for a moment before he shook his head and forced himself to focus. He had invoices to review before another meeting about the Super Bowl, the last massive event before Fourth of July madness turned the office upside down again. He glanced at his phone, reminding himself to sync his calendar, when he noticed a missed text from Armando.

Thanks for meeting up with Keira, man. She's been smiles all morning.

That news made Daniel's day. He had no idea what the hell he was doing with Keira, but this weird tightness in chest pulled even tighter at the thought of making her happy. He shot Armando a text back.

Not a problem. She's a great girl.

Just as he hit send, another text hit his phone, this one from Keira. It must be break time at the gym. Daniel pictured Keira and Armando standing around talking about him.

I Googled "switch".

That made him smile for sure.

Oh yeah? What did you find?

Naked people.

Is that all?

I got so caught up looking at all the naked people it was time for me to go to bed before I remembered my original plan.

Plan? Daniel was definitely intrigued. What was Keira up to?

Not telling. You'll laugh me into next week.

I won't. He wouldn't.

Well you said a switch does both.
I don't think I'd be good at submitting.
I was looking up how to be a good mistress.
I'll continue my research tonight.

Let me know if you need any assistance.

I will.
Also I'm not saying that I'm going to dominate you or anything.
I just like to know. I like to know things.

And now he was hard. He could imagine it so clearly, being under her control. It made him wonder though, what had changed, what had Keira suddenly considering domination and submission, any aspect of it, beyond her so-called quest for knowledge? Daniel adjusted the crotch of his jeans then started to text back, but Keira's next text beat him to it.

Knowledge is power. Followed by a toothy smiley face.

Daniel snorted with laughter. He'd only known her a few days, but he could imagine Keira saying those exact words, and the smile that came with it. Would she still be smiling when she got to know him though? Daniel wondered what she would think of his video collection. The hours and hours of footage he had of himself engaged in erotica acts. Some he'd uploaded to the internet for educational purposes, sharing them with friends. Hell, Armando had shared a few of his clips with Nailah when she was getting into the game. No, Keira wasn't ready for that. There was a good chance she never would be.

Daniel had sworn to Keira that he wouldn't back out of their plans, but now that he was thinking of who he really was and what he really needed, and how things between then would probably end, jumping ship before things got complicated might be for the best.

Wait. You guys are going out again? The text from Armando appeared at the top of the screen.

"What the fuck?" Daniel said out loud as he clicked over, reading the text again. He was not in the mood for this shit, not when he was this horny and frustrated. He pressed the little phone icon next to his friend's name. Armando answered right away.

"What's the problem, man?" Daniel said.

"Nothing. Hold on." Daniel waited while Armando probably took their conversation out of Keira's earshot. "I came in and she's talking to Grant about seeing you again and asking just how committed you are to kink and if she should date you and shit. What happened?"

"Nothing *happened*. We spent the day together and we had a good time. We want to see each other again."

"I just didn't think you guys would go out."

"I get that, but we are going out," Daniel said, his regret shifting somehow into determination.

"So what are you going to do, 'cause I just—"

"You just what?" Daniel laughed. He'd known Armando for years. He had always been a possessive Dom, but Keira wasn't his and Daniel wasn't his to push around either. He was not going to let this shit slide. "You know you have your own girlfriend right?"

"Fuck you. That's not what I was getting at. She's just vanilla, man. Extra strength vanilla. She's not ready for all of *you*."

"Let me be the judge of that. Shit, let her be the judge of that."

Daniel's phone beeped with another text from Keira. "I gotta go. Just be proud of the possible love connection you've helped facilitate."

This time Armando laughed. "Good luck, man. I hope you know what you're doing."

Yeah, me too, he almost said. How the fuck was this going to end well?

CHAPTER THREE

Despite his freezing cold feet, and Armando's odd, yet completely justified behavior, Daniel managed to nail down a date and time to see Keira again. At first they'd planned to go to the movies and out for some dinner, but she'd texted him that morning begging off for a night in. When she quickly clarified that she wasn't in fact cancelling, they decided on a movie and pizza at her place. He was buying.

On his way to pick up some beers, he got a text from his buddy, Marcos. Nothing official was planned at The Club that night, but Marcos was always up for something.

You busy tonight? I got some new tails.

After his accident, Daniel had gone through a long recovery period, learning to do a number of things with his left hand while his right arm healed. In the decade since, he'd become perfectly adept at functioning with both arms, with or without his prosthesis. But beyond healing, he'd become obsessed with perfecting his skills with a flogger. With hours spent practicing with Master Phillip, he'd crafted himself into somewhat of a legend in the community. He moved on to other implements; paddles, slappers, cat o' nine tails, bullwhips, canes. He'd taught classes and seminars, made plenty of videos, performed night after night at the club and in private for his Mistress and her Master. It was only natural for Marcos to reach out to Daniel when he'd acquired a new toy. Daniel was the best person to help him break it in.

Daniel read the backlit words again. Any other night he would have said yes. Had he made plans with any other girl he would have invited them along. But as curious as Keira was, what Marco had in mind would surely scare her off. A girl like Keira would need monogamy, for one. A girl like Keira would definitely need a little warm-up before he introduced her to his sexually fluid friends and their collection of whips and cat o' nine tails. He texted Marcos back.

Can't tonight, man. I made plans. Thanks for thinking of me though.

Something else stirred in his chest. First time in years he'd turned down an invite.

Always. Have a good night!

Oddly enough, even though he suspected their date would be vanilla and pretty tame, he had a feeling that spending a few hours just talking to Keira would make for a perfectly good night.

Keira had shown Daniel her nerdy side and clearly it hadn't scared him off or he wouldn't have agreed to see her again. Now she had a chance to show him another real side of herself, the lazy bum who hated getting dressed up for anything other than conventions. Her hair was already flat ironed, but that stayed in its ponytail. When she finished in the shower she'd thrown on an oversized Melrose Fitness sweatshirt and a pair of workout shorts that really could have doubled as underwear. She put on underwear too, including a bra, and she'd shaved her legs. She wasn't a complete heathen.

It was hard not to run for the door when the bell chimed through her apartment. She may have skipped though, and she did nothing to conceal the huge smile that hit her face when she opened the door for Daniel and the two large pizzas he carried.

"A veggie lovers and a meat lovers for the lady who does not like to mix the two."

Keira laughed as she let him in. "I'm sorry. I just like my meat separate."

"I'm sure you do. Here take these off my hands."

"Oh sure." Daniel had a leather jacket on, but Keira realized that he was wearing a prosthetic arm with a blunted hook he was using to carry a six-pack of amber ales. She took the pizzas then led him to the living room so they could make themselves comfortable in front of her TV. After she put down the pizzas she looked up at him.

"When I see a movie for the first time I demand silence, so I figured we could revisit some classics and let the running commentary flow. Dates should involve conversation, after all."

"I couldn't agree more." Daniel put down the beers and shed his leather jacket. "What?" he asked, with a slight grin.

"Sorry. I didn't mean to stare." Which she totally was. "It's just nice to see you."

"It is?"

"Yeah. I haven't really looked forward to seeing a guy in a while. It's nice."

"Well, here I am, in the flesh," he said with his gorgeous smile. "I hope tonight lives up to pleasant expectations."

Right then, Keira wanted to kiss him, but five minutes into their first date was all kinds of too soon. When they sat down she figured cuddling was off the table too. Ignoring the fact that cuddling had even entered her mind, she made herself comfortable on the other side of the couch with her feet tucked under her butt. Did a guy like Daniel even cuddle? Or if she wanted to get close to him would she have to get on the floor and play human footstool? Cuddling bondage style.

She really needed to get out of her head.

"How does *Terminator 2* sound?" she asked.

"One of my favorites. Let's do it."

Keira found the movie in the queue on her streaming service, then hit play. They dug into the pizza and polished off two beers each, sharing light conversation about work and the upcoming Terminator movie before resting back to actually watch the film. It was hard to take her eyes off Daniel, but as soon as the T-1000 popped on the screen she was back in nerd mode, reliving the excitement of the first time her aunt let her sneak and watch T2 on VHS with her cousins.

"Do you mind if I take this off? I've had it on all day." Keira looked over as Daniel started shrugging out of the straps that secured his prosthesis to his shoulders.

"Sure. Here." Keira hopped up and cleared a spot off the trunk behind her couch. Daniel stood and took the arm off, and then the white stocking that covered the healed area where his wrist should have been. Keira smiled as he let out a sigh that turned into groan as he rubbed his skin. It was strained relief, but to Keira it was an oddly pleasurable sound.

"Does it hurt? To wear the arm?" she asked when they sat back down.

"It doesn't hurt, but it likes to remind you that it's there. All the time. I usually only wear it to work or if I need to around the house. Uhh, that feels better and now I can do this."

Keira let out a little squeak when Daniel reached down and grabbed her legs. The squeak was followed almost immediately by a moan as he started rubbing her feet. Daniel worked the top of her foot and toes with his left hand and used his right arm to massage the arch and her heel. It wasn't a cuddling, but it was something.

"You have no idea how good that feels." Keira moaned as she slid down into the couch cushions.

"You're on your feet all day. I'm sure you could use a good rub down."

"Obviously. You don't have to stop at the feet. Really. I won't be mad if you want to do my whole body."

"You sure about that?"

"You know what I mean, pervert."

"How 'bout you just let me know when you're ready for me to go a little higher?"

"Oh, I will," Keira replied, almost so softly she wasn't entirely sure Daniel had heard her. She watched him for a few more moments out of the corner of her eye. He was wearing another simple t-shirt that was snug enough to show off the definition in his chest and his biceps, but somehow the perfect article of dark cotton didn't look tight. It made him look…delicious.

Keira spoke again on impulse. "What's your favorite thing, switch-wise?"

"Switch-wise?"

"What's your favorite 'activity'?"

"That's right. You never did tell me the results of your research. Is this a part of your Mistress plan? Slowly pull the information out of me after I'm fed and completely relaxed?"

Keira scoffed as she squirmed some more on her end of the couch. "At least one of us is relaxed."

Daniel immediately stopped the movements of his fingers. "Am I hurting your feet?"

"No, that's no—No. You can keep going with the foot thing. I was just wondering what you like. The stuff I found that was…sexual seemed to appeal to the general masses and then there were other things that just looked like something you would do to someone during an interrogation."

He kept on with her foot, but tilted his head back and looked thoughtfully at the ceiling. "Hmm, my favorite activity. That's a tough question. Sometimes it depends who I'm with, what they want, what kind of mood I'm in, what kind of mood they're in. With some people, it's been the same thing each time."

"Ah, I see." Keira needed to shut up. She was glad Daniel had come over, and he was aces with the whole foot rub thing, but no amount of internet research would prepare her for his other extracurricular activities. What she needed to do was enjoy her time with him. Enjoy the foot rub, enjoy the movie. Yes, she was curious. She'd been curious all week, but thinking about the freaky things Daniel liked to do for days on end was different from participating in those things with him. She was *not* ready, so why bring those freaky things up?

Damn right you're not ready, she told herself. Just watch the movie.

"With you?" Daniel said.

Keira's eyes opened wide the second she realized what he was getting at. Just as quickly she closed them and covered her ears. "No. Don't tell me. Please."

Daniel's deep laugh vibrated up her legs. "Why not? We're just talking. It's all hypotheticals."

"Because—" Keira lowered her hands. "Actually, no. Tell me."

"See, I can already tell that your thirst for knowledge will betray you every time. But let me think. With you, being the generous, thorough Mistress I know you can be, I think possibly a little edging, or some prostate milking. I'd have to be gagged though. And tied down."

"I understood about three-quarters of what you just said. What the heck is edging?"

"It's a way of being stimulated for a long period of time, without coming."

"How long are we talkin'?"

"Depends how much time you have? Schedule permitting, I've had sessions go all day."

"Wait someone played with your… your dick all day long? Like for a whole day and you didn't come?"

"I came eventually, but yes. We were at it for basically the whole day."

"Yeah, no. I don't think I could do that. My arms would get tired."

"There are ways to get creative. You don't have to use your hands at all."

Keira's brain almost broke as she tried to picture it. Daniel naked. Trying not to come. She coughed. "So you like edging, while being tied up and gagged. That's your favorite thing?"

"When I'm submitting, yeah."

"And when you're not?"

"Oh, I don't know. I love to eat pussy. I mean, I guess I like to do that when I'm submitting too, but if you were under me, I'd eat your pussy until you couldn't walk anymore and then I'd fuck you to sleep."

Keira swallowed in an attempt to calm her jumping nerves. This time when she squirmed, her feet shifted in Daniel's lap, right against what appeared to be his growing erection. She shouldn't have looked directly at his crotch, but she couldn't help it. She wasn't thinking clearly. When she looked up, Daniel was staring back at her. She had no idea what made her so bold but she moved her foot again, this time with meaning.

"All this, just from talking about it?" she asked.

"Mhmm. And thinking about you. You have to tell me now. What do you like?"

Keira realized she was wet now. She could feel the wet patch forming between her legs. "What do you mean?"

"I know you're not well versed in bondage or submission, but you've had sex and I'm guessing you masturbate. What's your sexual act of choice?"

Thinking of an answer was the distraction she needed. Daniel was still rubbing her foot, but now there was the matter of his hard-on and how the thickness of it was pressed against the side of her arch. She balled her fists in her sweatshirt to keep from slipping her own fingers a little farther down her body.

"I don't know. I just like sex."

"Sex covers a lot ground. Let's be more specific. What's a top fantasy of yours?"

"Ha. Finding a guy who's willing to sit through a Twilight Zone marathon with me at least three times a year."

"I'm sitting right here. Try again."

Keira rolled her eyes, but answered anyway. "I don't know. More foreplay, maybe. Every guy I've ever been with? We've done all sorts of positions, but we always get right to the sex. There's never any build up. Just, *Bam!* Doin' it. I was with one guy who didn't even kiss me. He just threw me on the bed and pulled my underwear off. I want, like, more—what's the word I'm looking for? I want more play, more fun. I want it to last longer, before it even gets started. I am making no sense."

"No, you're making complete sense. What's one thing you've always wanted to do with a partner that you haven't?"

"I'm going to tell you, but I want you to know it's super embarrassing to say all this out loud."

"There's no reason to be embarrassed. How can you get what you want if you don't share the details? Out with it."

"True. Okay. I really like watching guys jerk off. It's like the only porn I watch, when I watch porn." Keira said the words so fast it was like they all ran together.

"What do you like about watching guys jerk off?"

"I just think it's hot. I mean, porn's a mess, but when it's just one person it just seems more real. Less forced. A little less ridiculous. I've always thought it would be fun to watch a guy masturbate before or even after we have sex. He can watch me too, but yeah."

"So you like watching guys come?"

"You make it sound like I have a hole drilled in a men's locker room wall somewhere."

"Hey, I don't know what you do when you're at work. Excuse me." Daniel gently lifted her feet and placed them back on the couch. Then he reached for his zipper and started undoing his pants. It wasn't until his hand was all the way inside his boxers that Keira realized what he was doing.

"Oh my gosh, no! Don't!"

"You sure?" Daniel asked, his hand still in his boxers.

"No. Yes. I don't know! Do you usually whip it out on first dates?"

Daniel dropped his chin, giving her a telling look. "It's happened."

"Oh gosh. Okay. Okay. Do it. No! Do it."

"Okay. I'm gonna do it, but from now on if you really, genuinely don't want me to do something, say 'pizza'."

"Is that our safeword?"

Daniel's smile should be illegal in every state. "So you did do your homework."

"A little bit. Okay, pizza. That'll be your word too so I don't get confused. Not that you'll get anywhere near using it. I just—yeah. Okay. Do it. Oh my gosh. What we doing? There's still pizza left!" Keira blurted out the last bit just before she covered her eyes again. He was lifting his hips to give himself more room to pull his boxers and his jeans all the way down. She couldn't watch, but she had to. When Keira dared to peek between her fingers knew she had to stop him again.

"Wait! Kiss me first. Just real quick. If we're going to do anything close to sex, you have to kiss me. Makes it more personal, less… back room of the saloon."

"You're weird, but I like it. Here I come. I'm gonna kiss the shit out of you."

He wasn't kidding either. Daniel went for it, climbing over her, digging his fingers into her hair as he lightly caressed her cheek and then her neck with the healed skin on his arm.

Goose bumps had already spread out all over her body, but now her goose bumps had caught some sort of fever. His lips were so soft and he knew how to use the right amount of tongue at the right moment. Just a hint brushed against her own tongue, and then a little more.

He was pulling away before she knew it, back on the other end of the sofa with his jeans halfway down his thighs before she could tell him she wasn't done yet, but then his hand was in his boxers and he was pulling out his cock.

Keira was almost humiliated by how much it fascinated her. It was nice looking, as dicks go. Long and thick, which wasn't unfamiliar to Keira. She'd been with well-endowed guys before but, as Daniel started to stroke himself, it really hit Keira just how one note her sex life had been. If she could count the seconds, from kiss to the moments that followed—if it wasn't suggested that Keira enthusiastically give her partner some head—she never got a moment to appreciate a man's body.

If Daniel was anything like her last boyfriend, he'd already have her bent over the arm of the couch, going at her doggy-style and coming before she could even get close to her finish. Like clockwork, he'd go down on her afterward, but if she came, or if she faked it, he'd head to her room to pass out or take off for his own place before she could get her wits back. Her last boyfriend sucked.

But as she watched Daniel, his long fingers gliding over his skin, squeezing and tugging, she wanted to sleep with him, she wanted to take things further, but this was her fantasy, witnessing this filthy, private act. Why had it taken so long for her to find someone she could share her fantasies with?

"Can you take off your shirt?" she asked suddenly. "And your pants? All the way. Please."

"Yes, ma'am." His tone was light, but sincere. He stood up and started to shed his clothes. Keira almost asked if he needed a hand, but thought better of it. He deftly undressed one-handed and, even if he hadn't been able to manage, Keira got the feeling he would ask for help if he needed it.

When he sat back down, a look of concentration came over his face, like before maybe he had been teasing her, seeing how far he could go before she pizza'd their night to an early conclusion. Now the game was on.

"You have to tell me if you want me to stop, or if you want me to come," he said.

Keira pulled her knees up to her chest. "Definitely don't stop. I'll...I'll tell you when to come."

Daniel just nodded and kept on stroking.

The movie had long since faded into the background, but the sounds of the gunshots and motorcycle chases and explosions gave Keira something in the distance to focus on. She needed something tangible, an anchor to keep her from going wild as she watched him. She didn't want to think about what more she could want from this scenario, because Keira had no doubt in her mind that Daniel would give it to her.

She had no clue what he was talking about half the time they discussed anything sexual. She could come to him with the wildest, most off the wall idea and she knew he would have no problem meeting her demands. She was still playing in the minors, but guys like Daniel had invented the game, crafted the whole rulebook. Her most outrageous request would seem like child's play to him and that scared her.

"How do you do it when you're alone?" she managed to ask.

"Just like this, no alteration to the show."

"I mean what do you think about?"

"I think about how good it feels, touching my own cock. Or I think about something else that would make me come." Daniel's voice was strained in the sexiest way. Keira had a feeling he was getting close, but he would wait for her to say it was okay.

"Like what? What kinds of things make you come?"

"Right now? I'm thinking about you and if you enjoy watching me."

"I do. It's really hot."

"Then that's enough—Fuck." Daniel let his head fall back as he stroked himself faster. "Thinking about how much you like this is enough to make me go off."

Without really thinking, Keira braced herself on the couch and slid closer to Daniel, so close her knees were now pressed against his bare thigh. His head was still tilted back, but he cracked his eyes open just a bit to look at her. He licked his lips.

Kiera leaned in a little more. "Can I touch you?"

"You don't have to ask."

"Yes, I do. Don't stop." Keira meant to lead with her hands, but her mouth took charge. She kissed Daniel on his shoulder, leaning a little closer so her lips could make the journey along his neck. He smelled so good. Something clean, but warm and fresh, like fabric softener and the hint of a perfect cologne. His arm brushed against her breasts as his hand kept on moving up and down his shaft.

He turned his head just enough and their lips met, but Keira pulled away. Before, it had been clear that she wanted the kissing portion of the night to go on and on, but now she knew what would happen if they kept kissing and she wanted to save that for another time.

Daniel seemed to understand. He slowed his movements down again, squeezing his cock in his palm, alternating his grip, upside and then down, probably to keep himself from coming before she said it was okay. Keira laid her head on the back of the couch and continued to watch. Her knees were still pressed against his thigh.

After a few minutes of listening to his harsh breathing and occasional groans, Keira couldn't take anymore.

"You should come now," she said, her voice near a whisper.

It didn't even take a second suggestion or a couple more pumps of his fist. Come erupted out of Daniel's cock and onto his stomach. It came in several jets, a creamy white, painting his lightly honeyed skin. The sounds that came out of him were just as erotic as the sight of his fingers urging the last drops from his swollen head. He continued to touch himself until he was completely finished, but Keira knew she was still in charge. She still owned the moment. In her fantasy, in some of the better clips she'd watched, this had always been her favorite part.

"I like it when guys spread it around."

"Like this?" Daniel said, using his fingertips to move what he'd spilled on his stomach across his defined abs and up the center of his chest.

"Lower."

Daniel followed orders and spread what was left farther down, up the length of his penis and around his balls. He was still breathing a little heavy, but Keira could tell he wanted more. It would be wrong for her to pretend that she didn't too, but there was no clear direction for her to go. Her own body was still tingling. She'd soaked through her underwear and there was no doubt in her mind that if she slid her hand between her legs she'd find that her shorts were wet too.

But part of her wanted to hold on to that tight, swollen sensation, the heat. It would be easy to tell him to go down on her, or to tell him to rally up another hard-on so they could have sex. Either of those things could happen, or both, but she was practically high off the control, off of her own arousal. An orgasm would ruin that for her.

"Tell me what you want."

Keira thought about it for a moment before she answered. "Can you spend the night, just like this? No clean up?"

"Okay."

"Do you want to finish watching this in my room?"

"That would be nice."

"Wait here one sec." Keira grabbed the remote and turned off the TV, then put away the rest of the pizza. Then she told Daniel to follow her down the hall. She glanced back at him as they went. His cock was softening, but it still had some life to it. In her bedroom, she pulled back the sheets and invited him to lie down. She could feel his eyes on her as she set about getting ready for bed. She ditched her sweatshirt and her shorts, and grabbed her laptop before she climbed between the sheets with him in just her bra and underwear.

"You want me just like this?" he asked.

Keira looked back over her shoulder at him, realizing that no one had pizza'd. She was still in charge. He was lying in the same spot, back against her pillows, legs slightly spread.

Rolling over, she considering him for a minute. Was there more to the fantasy? What did she really want?

"Um, how do you feel about spooning?"

"It's something I enjoy."

"Okay, you be the big spoon please."

Daniel didn't hesitate to scoot closer and wrap his arm around Keira's stomach. She moved back and down a little as well, pressing her ass against his crotch as she loaded the video streaming to the spot where they'd left off. It didn't take long before he was hard again.

It was difficult not to wonder what would happen on their second date.

CHAPTER FOUR

"Was last night weird?"

Daniel looked up at Keira, who was still cozy in her bed. It was early as hell, still dark out, but work called. Still, he couldn't help but smile as he slung his harness and arm into place. "That wasn't even close to weird. That was hot. I will happily jerk off for you any time."

"Not the jerking off part. I mean everything else."

Daniel had to admit, Keira had surprised him. Coming for her was a breeze, but he hadn't expected the rest, her wanting him in her bed, on her fresh sheets, covered in his own jizz. Some of it got on her back when she asked him to spoon her, but that wasn't the last of it.

As they watched the rest of the movie, she started to rub her soft ass against his hard cock. He'd held still, letting her wiggle and grind against him as she pleased, thinking maybe this was her way of getting off, but that wasn't the case. Eventually she asked him if he could come again, just from rubbing up his cock along her ass. Of course he could and he told her as much, but he still waited until she told him to rub himself off again, using only her ass for friction. The idea alone brought his hard-on completely back to life and, in seconds, he had her small, tight body pulled flush against him as he rotated his hips. This time she let him touch her, guiding his hand up over her breasts. He pulled the thin cotton of her bra aside and teased her puckered nipples until she told him to climax again. Which he did, all over her back and ass.

He could have sworn he heard her moan and knew he felt her shiver a bit, but he knew there was more. Still, she just wanted him to hold her, no reciprocation, no clean up. Had someone asked him where he saw their night going, his answer would not have included him lying naked in her bed after she'd exhibited a bit of a jizz fetish, but, on the scale of a little off to this chick needs help, what Keira wanted from him fell right on par with normal. She liked what she liked and Daniel was honored to be the one she'd opened up to.

"If you're looking for someone to judge you, you're looking at the wrong guy. Nothing we did last night was weird. If we step outside of my comfort zone, I will tell you. And I hope you'll do the same."

"Good to know."

It was beyond time for him to go. He had a ton of shit to do to prepare for the wedding that night. A wealthy groom wanted to end the couple's exchange of vows with a two minute fireworks display. He insisted that Daniel be there to oversee the crew, even though his team was more than capable. Either way, the client was always right and he had to be at the venue early. That didn't change the fact Daniel wasn't quite ready to leave Keira yet. He grabbed his jacket, but climbed back onto the bed. His slid his hand under the covers and up her bare thigh. Her skin was so soft, so smooth. "Are you sure you don't want me to take care of you?"

"I'm sure. Maybe I want you to work for it," Keira said with a smile.

"I like the sound of that. When can I see you again?"

"Whenever you want. My schedule's busy, but it's pretty regular. Yours seems more action packed."

"How about I call you?"

"And I'll text you in the meantime?"

"You better." And then, like it was almost an automatic response, Daniel closed the small space between them and kissed Keira one last time.

"I'll see you," he said. And then he kissed her again.

"'Kay."

Daniel had to force himself off the bed and out the door. He was still pretty high from the orgasms he had the night before, not to mention waking up with Keira still in his arms. He walked out to his SUV, checking his cell as he hit the curb. He'd missed a couple calls and there were a few texts. The calls and messages were from Mike. Just a few reminders about the day, a message asking if Daniel had walked off with his favorite socket wrench, and a final message saying he found it. Mike really needed to learn to utilize the text feature on his cell.

The texts were all from Mistress Evelyn.

Hey Honey. You free later?
Meegan earned a reward.
I was hoping you could come over and help me treat her.

The texts tripped Daniel up in the most unexpected way. He climbed behind the wheel and stared at his phone. The regret was back. Seeing Keira again, spending the night with her, that all felt right, but he hadn't given any thought to what would happen after. He hadn't considered what the fuck he should do when his life came calling. Or texting, in this case. Any other time, his response to Mistress

Evelyn would be an automatic yes, but his fingers refused to type out that simple word. He was starting to feel something for Keira and the idea of being with someone else without her knowing, even if there was nothing romantic about it, didn't sit well with him. He had a feeling it wouldn't sit well with Keira either.

Actually I don't think I can make it. Daniel texted back. Mistress Evelyn was an early riser. She'd probably been up since 4:30, embracing the quiet as she got her day started.

She sent a text right back.

Something up? You never miss a chance to play with me and the girls.

This wasn't the conversation to have over text. Daniel hit the little phone icon next to Mistress Evelyn's name.

"Hey, sweetheart. What's going on?"

He got right to the point. "I've kind of just started seeing someone and she's not in the community."

"Oh." Daniel wasn't quite sure how to read her shock, but her tone quickly became more pleasant, less what-the-fuck. "I'm sorry, honey. I wasn't expecting you to say that. Tell me about her."

Daniel told her pretty much everything that had happened since he and Keira had met on more official terms. He didn't realize he was rambling on about her laugh and her smile and the blunt, yet innocent and honest ways she carried on conversations until he heard Mistress Evelyn's laugh through his phone.

"What?"

"Nothing. It's just—you two sound like me and Philip when we first met. We didn't have all the text messaging back then, but he proposed to me after a week."

"Well, we aren't even close to that. I just like her."

"I know honey, but it's been a short time and it sounds like she's already changing you. And not in a bad way."

"Changing me how?" Daniel didn't like the way that sounded.

"Well, when was the last time you told me no? And I've never heard you go on about anyone like this. About things, yes, but never people. I just never—"

"Pictured me dating a vanilla girl?"

"Not exactly. I just didn't know if you would ever want to settle down."

Daniel closed his eyes. "We're not settling down. We're hanging out. I just I think she needs monogamy right now."

"What do you need?"

The honest answer to that question scared the shit out of him, so for the first time ever, he lied to Mistress Evelyn.

"I don't know. Time to think?"

"Well, you take all the time you need. Phillip and I will always be here for you."

"Yeah, I know," Daniel said, feeling like a complete asshole. "I know."

Keira's last cardio kickboxing class was going down in slow flames. Saturday mornings were always the best. Everyone who had slacked during the week, or just didn't have time, showed up in droves for Armando's first yoga session and Grant's boot camp. She had her a.m. regulars, but 5:30pm on Saturdays were where workouts went to die. She often had to cancel her last class, but one of her clients decided to show up with three of her friends, who actually had no interest in working out.

Keira had to push them though. It was her job.

"Hands up, ladies. There you go. Keep going," she called out over the music. "And five. Four. Three. Two. One. Now step. And punch. Good! Step. And punch." She'd punch herself in the face of she could.

Before she could manage it, the front doors eased open and Daniel poked his head in. Keira almost lost her count. She smiled like a fool though, so big that Jan, the one putting in the least amount of effort, actually stopped her stepping and punching to see what she was looking at.

"Come on, Jan. Stay with us. Five. Four…"

Keira nodded toward the back and mouthed "Armando." Daniel got the drift and made his way back to the office where Armando was probably busy sexting his girlfriend.

The last ten minutes of the class dragged on forever. Finally she wrapped things up and sent Jan and company off to no doubt complain about what a horrible mistake they'd made taking her class. Once they were gone, Keira darted to the back office.

"Hey! What happened to the wedding?" she asked Daniel. He was leaning against the wall in the packed space.

"Bride left the groom at the altar."

"Ouch." Armando grimaced.

"Oh my god," Keira added.

"Yeah, we offered to stay for the guests, but they pulled the plug on the whole thing. So here I am."

"You're free tonight?" Keira asked, as she bounced on her heels. It had barely been twelve hours since she'd last seen him, but when he left her place that morning she was convinced it would be another week before she actually got to see him again. She couldn't hide her excitement. Daniel time was A+ quality time.

"It seems so. Would you like to go out?"

"Yes. Oh, I know. Let's go play some skeeball. There's this place called The Alley Way—"

"That doesn't sound suspect at all," Daniel said with a smile. Then he motioned her closer. "Come here."

"I'm kinda sweaty."

"I don't care."

Keira walked into his arms and stood up on her tiptoes so she could kiss this man that she was suddenly dying to call her boyfriend. Their smooch lasted just long enough for it to be awkward with another person in the room. When they broke apart, Keira looked over to see Armando staring at them in the most bizarre way.

"What's that look?" she asked.

Armando fixed his face and tried to play it off like he hadn't just looked completely disgusted. "Ah- nothing. I—"

But Daniel wasn't letting him off that easily. "He thinks me showing up here is a sign that we're moving too fast."

"Well, then he shouldn't have introduced us. Two dates in two nights too out of control for you, Mando?" Keira laughed. She turned around in Daniel's arms and made herself comfortable. He pulled her closer and Keira could have sworn she saw Armando cringe.

"Nope, not at all," Armando said. "I didn't say a word."

"What are you and Nailah doing tonight? You want to come with us?" Daniel suggested.

"Yeah, you can chaperone. Make sure things don't get too out of hand in the fun department," Keira added.

"Can't. I promised her a thing."

"I'm sure you did." Keira looked over her shoulder. "Just us tonight?"

Daniel hugged her tighter. "Just us."

★

In forty short minutes they were kicked out of The Alley Way. When they arrived, Keira headed right for the skeeball machines, and everything was going smoothly until Daniel decided to show Keira the way he and JD used to cheat. She knew the methods, but he insisted it was the fastest way to win her a giant stuffed panda that looked like it had been sitting behind the counter since the place opened in 1978.

They were in good shape when Daniel was just standing near the top of the ramp feeding balls into the 50 point hole, but the manager was about done when Daniel actually climbed up the ramp and made a dramatic show of slam-dunking their last ball into the hole while screaming "Ah yeah!" at the stop of his lungs.

Keira could not stop laughing. Even after they were closed in Daniel's SUV, they were both still cracking up. She had tears running down her face.

"I don't know what the fuck his problem was. He didn't have to be so pissed." The mock outrage in Daniel's tone made Keira laugh even harder.

"I know! Even after we gave all our tickets to those kids." Keira wiped her face. "Oh, my gosh, he's gonna ban me for life. What do we do now? It's not even 8:30."

"It's your call, sweetheart."

"I don't know. Let's just go back to your place." Keira was half laughing when she said it. It took a few seconds for her to notice that Daniel wasn't laughing anymore. He was just looking at her. "Or...we don't have to?"

Daniel shook his head a little. "No, sorry. I think I just heard you the wrong way. Actually that's not right. Old habits run deep or however you want to say it. Usually when I have people to my place, things go a certain way. You saying we should go there, it triggered something."

Keira's case of the giggles was definitely gone. "What way is a certain way?"

"If we go back to my place you're agreeing to submit to me. For the night."

"I have to do whatever you want?"

"No. We'll talk about what I want to do to you and what I want you to do with me and if we both agree, then we will spend the night doing those thing."

Keira was confused. That sounded like regular consensual sex. "I don't get it."

"This isn't about me just bossing you around. You relinquish control, trusting that I'm going to give you exactly what you need. At the same time, your desire to please me, if you have that desire, will naturally lead to you doing things that please me."

"Like what?"

"Like letting me taste you. Letting me find out what you feel like inside. I'm also going to come on your tits. That's definitely gonna happen."

"Those sound like things that would please me."

"Hmm," was all Daniel said.

"What? What did I say wrong?"

"You didn't say anything wrong. I'm just getting a clearer picture of what you think is happening here. It is possible for me to find pleasure in pleasuring you. We can want the same things. It wasn't like that with your exes, I'm guessing."

"No, you're right. It was always this sort of tit for tat thing. I always had to hope and bargain and beg—"

"And you were still left unsatisfied."

"Yeah."

"I think we need to change that. You still want to go to my place?"

Keira didn't hesitate. Her answer was yes. The night before had been nothing like any first date she'd ever experienced, but she wouldn't change a thing about it. She liked Daniel. She trusted him. It might be fun to see what it was like if the tables were turned.

"Let's get out of here, then. I'd rather not fuck you in my car."

"What if it pleases me though?"

"Well, if you insist." Keira practically screeched with laughter as Daniel started undoing his fly and climbing over the center console in almost the same motion.

"Oh my gosh! Can't you wait?"

Daniel settled back in his seat and looked over at her. "I'm just following orders."

"That wasn't an order. It was a… a question."

"Sorry."

Keira glared back at him "No you aren't."

"Forgive me?"

"Only if we stop and get ice cream before we go back to your place."

"Deal. Let's go." Keira watched as Daniel hit the PUSH START button with the side of his smooth hook. Butterflies started a full dance party in her stomach as they pulled out into traffic. What had she just agreed to?

CHAPTER FIVE

They pulled up to a brand-new, modern style house in Atwater Village. Keira asked Daniel about the neighborhood and he told her when he'd decided to buy instead of renting, as she followed him through the side door into the kitchen. Daniel put the two pints of ice cream—vanilla for comfort and cinnamon bun just in case they were feeling adventurous—in the freezer. Then he turned toward her.

"Okay." Keira bounced on the balls of her feet. As if it wasn't obvious enough that she was nervous. "What do I do first?"

"I want you to take off your clothes. Everything."

"Are you going to watch?"

"Mhmm."

"Okay. Here goes. I'm getting naked. Can I talk while I get naked?"

"Mhmm."

"Good, 'cause I'm not very good at not talking," she said, as she pulled off her jacket.

"I know."

"Jerk." Her boots and socks were next.

"Keep going."

"I'm going." Her thin sweater and her shirt hit the floor. Then her jeans. "They added the latest season of *Galaxis* online. I'm going to do a re-watch sometime next week. You in?"

"Yes. If you take off your underwear, yes."

"Here. Underwear's off." Her bra and panties joined the pile.

"Thank you. I'll be right back."

Daniel left Keira standing naked in the middle of his kitchen. She glanced around, but there wasn't all that much to see. The place was so new, it looked barely lived in. Or maybe Daniel didn't spend a whole lot of time in the kitchen. There was nothing on the walls, not even a reminder hanging on the fridge. The only thing that stuck out was a half-finished puzzle that seemed to dominate the kitchen table, what looked like a millions pieces that would eventually come together to make a depiction of a stained glass window featuring the Virgin Mary and Baby Jesus.

Daniel came back just as Keira was about to pick up one of the loose pieces. She spun around, caught in the act. "Sorry."

"It's okay. I've done that one a few times."

"So you weren't joking about the puzzles?" Keira said with a smile. This was the side of Daniel she wanted to get to know. She knew the man who liked to play with fire, literally, but it almost made her giggle to think of him settling in with a warm cup of tea to unwind with a one of his favorite puzzles.

"Not exactly. I had to learn how to use my left hand after my accident. The puzzles helped with my dexterity. I'll show you my drafting table later. I've become quite the left handed calligrapher."

"Ooh, I want to see that now."

"No. I want to play with you now."

Keira made a dramatic show of frowning at him, but that only lasted the few seconds it took for her to remember that she was butt naked and Daniel was going to show her what it was like to submit for him, on his terms.

He had a roll of red shiny tape hanging off his prosthetic hook. "Do you know what this is?"

"Festive duct tape?"

"It's called bondage tape."

"I'm probably ruining the mood, not being serious."

"No. You like to be silly and I like that about you."

"Oh."

"I'm going to bind you, wrists and feet. I'm going to cover your mouth and then I'm going to take you into my bedroom and we're going to have some fun."

"Promise you won't kill me."

"Keira."

"Promise."

Daniel leaned down and looked her right in the eyes. "I'm not going to kill you, I promise."

"I'm just saying, this is how horror movies start. I appreciate a bit of reassurance."

"I'm pretty sure Grant and Armando would be a little upset with me if didn't send you back to the gym happy and whole."

"That's true."

"Anyway. Can you snap?"

"My fingers? Yeah." Keira demonstrated, making a show of doing a little jig while she snapped both her fingers.

"Good. Instead of a safe word you're gonna snap. Place your hands behind your back, wrists crossed," He said the last bit as he circled her body. "And I want your feet together. Good, just like that." He made quick work securing her hands, then came back around to her front and got on his knees to secure her feet.

Keira tried to keep quiet and just observe as Daniel bound her ankles with the tape, but she was too nervous to stand there in silence. "I'm nervous," she blurted out.

Daniel glanced up at her, giving her the brief instance of reassurance she needed. "Why are you nervous?"

"Why shouldn't I be?"

"Because you're with me and I think you know I would never do anything to hurt you. I think you can infer that I'm not the type to hurt anyone."

"It's not that. I just, I'm not good at this."

"At what, Keira?"

Keira let out a deep sigh as Daniel finished with her feet. The way she felt didn't make any sense. She wanted to sleep with Daniel, even though she wasn't exactly sure sex itself was on the menu, but she wanted to be with him again. She was already naked and she did trust him. In the short time they'd spent together, Daniel had already proved to be one of the sweetest men she had ever met. She felt totally safe with him. And he might have been a little impulsive, trying to drop his pants at the slightest suggestion, but he always backed off, even if she wasn't completely sure she wanted him to stop. Plus she could always snap or pizza her way out of the situation. It wasn't

Daniel, it was something else she couldn't put into words, but it made her nervous as hell.

He stood and gently stroked her cheek. "Talk to me. What's wrong?"

"I'm scared."

"You're not used to being this vulnerable?"

"No, I'm not." The problem was Keira didn't hate it. She liked being naked for Daniel and she wanted to see what he had planned for the rest of the night. But that didn't change the fact that her heart felt like it was going to beat right through her chest. And she didn't like the idea of not being able to touch him. And, on the other hand, she didn't want him to untie her. Why was submitting so freaking confusing?

Daniel leaned down and kissed her. That cleared up some of the confusion. "Do you want to stop? We don't have to do this."

"No. I want this. I'm sorry. I'm just…"

"Let's try it for two minutes and after two minutes I'll check in with you and we'll see how you feel. No pressure to snap or anything."

"And you're still going to gag me? Cause you don't want me to talk the whole time?"

"I'm going to gag you because I want you to see what it feels like to experience something without being able to comment until it's finished. So what do you say? You want to try?"

Keira nodded, then added, "Yes." She wasn't sure what else she could say. She wanted to be with Daniel and she wanted to try something new. Fear came with the unknown sometimes and she was just going to have to deal.

Daniel wound a strip around Keira's face once, covering her mouth, then dipped down and threw her over his shoulder. For some weird reason as he carried her down the hall to his room, Keira started to pretend that she was being kidnapped. And for some even weirder reason it was the idea of being kidnapped—not being naked, not Daniel's kiss, but the thought of being taken by force, to be used by some strange man—that made her wet. She closed her eyes and pretended to accept her fate, stifling a small giggle as they made their way down the hall.

Daniel had taken the whole ride from the arcade to get his mind right, but Keira had tripped him up with all her chatter. Most of the submissives he'd played with had been trained by Master Philip and Mistress Evelyn. A few had been whipped into shape by

Armando. They were all different. All had their quirks, but none of them talked as much as Keira. He didn't mind all her talking, not at all. The problem was that listening to Keira talk took him out of his headspace, because when he should have been handling business he just wanted her to keep on jabbering. Her ridiculousness had made him laugh, it kept him guessing. He loved her energy. He could easily sit around talking to her all night, but he really, really wanted to have sex with her. At the very least he had to make her come.

When they reached his bedroom he made a decision. He initially considered taking things easy on Keira. She was already bound, wrists and ankles. Her mouth was covered so she couldn't say a word. In some ways that might be enough for her first night playing the role of submissive, but he had to give her more. He wasn't going to go nuts and take things all the way to the edge, but he needed to push her a little more, see if he could reach a place where he could at least see the edge far off in the distance. He gently laid Keira on the bed on her side. She was breathing normally, if not a little heavier than usual. He took a moment to remove his arm. It helped with the tape, and he'd had submissives ask for some of his other attachments, but *he* wanted full skin-to-skin contact.

Once he had everything he needed in place, he sat on the bed beside his captive, right in the curve her stomach created as her body bowed forward. He picked up the shears he had on the nightstand. Keira's eyes bulged wide. "Emergency precaution if we need to get the tape off quickly." Her shoulders sagged and she nodded. Daniel shook his head as he put the scissors back.

It was time to get down to business. Daniel knelt beside the bed but, just as he was about to pull Keira close, she started thrashing and making a noise that sound like his name. For a moment he thought she'd forgotten about her snap signal, but there was something a little too mischievous about the glint in her eye. And then it looked like she was trying to smile.

"Jesus Fucking Christ." It took a second, but he got Keira upright on her knees, then unwound the tape around her mouth. "What?"

"I don't care what you say. My father doesn't negotiate with terrorists," Keira said dramatically, before she bit the inside of her lips and made this little snorting noise.

"Nope. No way."

"Why?"

"My house, my rules. We can do your whole kidnapping, Stockholm syndrome fantasy at your place. Right now we're going to do things my way."

"I want to argue about this some more, but when you're firm like that it makes me really horny."

"Good. Tape's going back on." Daniel ignored her pouting, pushing her over on the bed as soon as the tape was back in place. He had planned to start with her tits, suck on them a while, just to help her get her mind focused on what was actually happening, but that wasn't going to work. She was distracting herself *and* him. Daniel was done wasting time. He dropped down on the bed and was not gentle about pulling Keira over his lap.

"I'm going to spank you now. Snap once if you want me to stop."

Keira's back rose and fell as she let out a deep breath, but her fingers remained still.

"Excellent. If you squirm I'm only going to make this worse."

Famous last words.

The spanking started off well enough. Not to say that anything went particularly wrong. It was just that, once again, Keira reacted in a way Daniel had not expected. He got in one, maybe two licks and then she started to squirm in his lap. She wasn't in pain, he could tell, and she wasn't even close to signalling out of the scene. It was the warning he'd given her. He'd taken away her fantasy so she was going to get a certain level of manhandling out of him by testing to see if his warnings were actually idle threats. He hadn't expected her to go there, but he was ready. He gave her ten hard licks, pausing briefly a few times to rub and grope at her luscious ass cheeks and thighs. She continued to squirm and moan, and squirmed and moaned some more when he stopped and slid his hand between her legs.

She was wet, coating his hand with her slickness as he pushed two fingers nice and deep.

"You want me to stop?"

She shook her head wildly.

"Good cause you're gonna have to beg me to stop."

Another moan, more desperate and pleading.

The spanking had worked for her, Daniel thought. He knew she could take more.

Daniel pulled his fingers out of Keira's soaked cunt, then dropped her back onto the bed. More groans and moans, but she rolled into the exact position he needed her in, on her side. He kneeled beside the bed and got her ponytail in the tight hold of his fist.

"How are we doing?" he said in a harsh voice. His promised check-in was a few minutes late. She glanced at him, but didn't make a noise. Air puffed out of her nose. "Do you want me to stop?"

She shook her head as much as he would allow. "Very good. I hope you're comfortable. You're gonna be like that for a while."

Keira made a little squeaking noise, but Daniel ignored her and went right for her nipple. He'd touched her breasts the night before, but he wanted a chance to really admire her body. Her breasts were perfect. A perfect handful with dark tips that been hard since the moment he told her to strip. He stroked over one tip with his tongue before pulling it between his lips. She squirmed again, but he still had a good grip on her hair.

He looked up at her face. Little wisps of dark brown were starting to curl around her forehead. "Are you trying to get away?" Dammit, Daniel thought. He'd played into her little game. Oh well. He was enjoying himself too much to stop. He lightly tugged her hair again. "Are you?"

Another shake of her head.

"I know what you need." Daniel stood unzipped his fly. "Maybe you'll hold still after I give you what you really want."

He pulled out his cock and gripped it as he stepped closer to the bed. "Get on your back, now."

Keira groaned, but she maneuvered her way into the perfect position for Daniel to straddle her stomach. The act of lying on her bound arms thrust her chest up. Still, it gave her a perfect view of his dick. He pulled up his shirt and tucked it under his chin, then started beating off.

Keira writhed, trying to arch closer to him.

"Open your eyes," Daniel barked. That got her attention. From then on she kept her eyes open, though she continued to struggle against the tape. He should have recorded this. He hadn't told Keira about his cinematic hobbies yet, but he wanted more than the memory of this night to recall. He wanted to watch it again and again in stark color. He wanted to see it from a different angle. See himself on top of this beautiful woman, see the way her well defined muscles corded under her beautiful brown skin as she ached for the come he was about to give her. They'd do this again, Daniel thought. He made up his mind about it, but the next time he'd bind her ankles to her thighs, strap her upper arms back, not just her wrists. He'd skip the gag though, the next time he was definitely coming in her mouth.

That made him go off; the sound of her moans, the look in her eyes, and the thought of him leaving a white trail along her pink tongue.

He managed to stay upright as he shot his load all over her stomach and her tits. Keira lost it, started thrashing about. She wanted to participate. She wanted to touch him, she wanted to spread his jizz around, but that wasn't part of Daniel's game. He squeezed the last bit of come out of his cock, the head red and swollen in his fist. Then he hopped off the bed and rolled Keira back onto her side so she was nearly teetering on edge of the mattress.

She was so far gone, forgetting his instructions the moment he shoved his fingers back between her legs. Two fingers deep in her wet cunt and his thumb pressing against her clit. "Look at me, baby. You're gonna come for me."

Keira shook her head. There were tears lining her eyes, but there was also desperation. She needed to see this scene to its completion.

Daniel leaned down and made a show of licking a bit of come off her nipple. He made sure she saw the white drops before he pulled them into his mouth and licked his lips.

"I'm gonna clean you up and you're gonna come for me."

Another wild moan as she squeezed her eyes shut, but he knew she couldn't stand to miss the show. He made his way down her chest and up again, licking and sucking up every trace of the mess he'd made. Daniel was no stranger to his own flavor, but he knew this was a first for Keira. When he glanced up she was watching him intently. He shook his fingers inside her and pressed harder on her clit. Her body was clenching around him, wanting so badly to just reach that peak, but Keira was fighting it and she would until she physically couldn't stand any more. That was fine with Daniel. He could wait. He had all the time and forearm strength in the world.

But it didn't take all that. Something in Keira snapped and she stopped fighting. Her whole body went tight, her legs straightening out on the bed, trapping his hand between her thighs as her head and her neck arched back. The sound she made came from her chest, maybe even deep in her stomach. She held it for a few long seconds before she sagged limply on the bed. But Daniel wasn't done. His slid in another finger, then the fourth. Her body opened up for him. He saw the muscles on her stomach flutter. Her eyes blinked open.

"Do you want me to stop?"

She shook her head no, even though tears were leaking from her eyes. Daniel knew that feeling. She'd found her space, the sub space they called it. There were all sorts of psychological ways of explaining it, but Daniel knew it as the point where he could finally let go, the moment where he found his safety wrapped in euphoria and it was no longer necessary for him to keep up the barriers and walls necessary to keep him safe in everyday life. Keira was there with him. She'd succumbed to all the sensations. She'd given in to the act of submission and now all she had to do was sit back and enjoy. Daniel had everything in hand, quite literally.

His thumb was the last to enter her warm cunt. He held still for a moment as she swirled her hips, feeling her muscles squeeze down on his fingers before they relaxed then tensed again.

Daniel moved his hand, his whole arm, with deep, pumping thrusts. His right arm, with its healed scars, traced over the skin of her breasts and nipples. Keira met him at every beat, harder and harder as her strength came back to her, until she climaxed again. It was different this time, not one hard explosion, but a series of mini eruptions. She lay trembling on her side as liquid leaked from between her thighs and onto the sheets. The sight of it, the watery proof of her pleasure, almost made Daniel come in his jeans.

Eventually he slid his fingers free. He went to the kitchen and, when he returned with a bottle of water, he quickly unwrapped the tape from Keira's mouth and cut the tape from her wrists and ankles. He wiped her face with a damp cloth he had waiting, then pulled her onto his lap and helped her take a sip of the water.

She looked up at him, the tears flowing more freely. It had been an intense hour.

"How are you feeling?" he asked.

"No small talk. Where's the ice cream?"

"Yes small talk. That's how this works. How are you feeling?"

Keira looked down and grabbed onto his t-shirt. "Is it okay if I can't put it into words? I feel a lot, or I felt a lot, but I don't know how to explain it."

"Yeah, that's very okay. Are you hurt anywhere?" She'd be sore in the morning just from struggling against the bindings, but he needed to know if he'd hurt her.

Keira took another sip of water then settled against his body. "I feel great. My brain is like pudding, but my body feels… I can't explain it."

"I get it."

"Good. Now ice cream. I need it."

"If I didn't love you so much I'd drop your ass on the floor right now."

"I know it's tough," Keira said, playing off his ill-timed declaration. "I love me too."

Daniel rolled his eyes, but gently moved her over to the pillows. He'd think about what he'd just let slip later. Much later. Way after ice cream.

"Daniel. Daniel."

He knew he wasn't alone. In fact he knew he'd fallen asleep with this perfect woman resting in his arms. Daniel just wasn't sure if he was dreaming or if Keira was really saying his name. He felt a little nudge to his ribs. "Dan."

"Yeah, babe."

"Do you have any condoms?"

"Yeah, I—"

She interrupted his sleepy groan. "I want to have sex with you."

He was still half asleep, but that was all his body needed to hear. He stood up and found the condoms in his dresser with his eyes nearly closed. Slid one on in an automatic motion. He was between her thighs next, feeling his way in the dark until his cock was exactly where in it needed to be. Keira bore down on him with a whimper, taking his whole length at once. He groaned in kind. She was so warm. Welcoming. There was no rush to come, just the slow, lazy motion of their bodies moving together. Daniel wanted it to last forever. He buried his face in the curve of her neck, praying it would.

CHAPTER SIX

Daniel set his menu down the moment he saw Mistress Evelyn glide into the restaurant. As she got closer he did what he been taught to do for the last ten years. He stood and pulled out her chair. She smiled and kissed him on the cheek.

"Hello, sweetheart. It's good to finally see you."

"Likewise." It had only been three weeks, but that was a long time when it came to being away from The Club and The Family.

Daniel took his seat, feeling his face heat for a few different reasons. It was always something to be around Evelyn. And Philip. But his Mistress definitely had a way about her that made you aware of everything. It was her voice, the light and smooth, delicate way of it, and the fact that she was easily six feet tall. She was over sixty, but black women age in that way that had most people convinced she wasn't a day over forty. She was beautiful, with her salt-and-pepper hair shaved close to her head. And all Daniel could think of was Keira. He looked down at his glass of water.

"Do we bother with the pleasantries or should we just talk?"

Daniel smiled. She knew him too well. "Whatever pleases you."

"Oh stop it. Tell me about her."

"I don't think I can." That was the only way to put it. Talking to Mistress Evelyn was always an easy thing to do. She'd been with him since the beginning. Seen him through rehab and physical therapy. She'd flown his mother down so she could be there when he was fitted for his first prosthesis. If he could confide in anyone, it was Mistress Evelyn Baker. But there was some sort of block when it came to Keira. He didn't like talking about her to anyone. It had nothing to do with shame. He loved her. He had admitted that to himself days ago. It was something closer to privacy. Something inside of him just didn't want to go there. But Mistress Evelyn wasn't giving up. She reached out and took Daniel's hand.

"Try. I want to know about this woman who's kept you away from us for so long."

Daniel gave up and pulled out his phone, going right to one of the many, many pictures of Keira he now had on it. A selfie she'd taken of them together the night before when she was sitting on his lap, live tweeting *Galaxis*. He handed his phone over.

"I thought you would have met her before at one of Grant or Armando's things, but I'm sure you would both remember each other."

"You told her about me?"

"Not exactly." More like not at all.

Mistress Evelyn just laughed. She was a stern, challenging Dominant, but also a kind, lighthearted, wonderful friend and Daniel was being an ass.

"Oh, she's beautiful. Such a sweet face, but I want to know, what's got you scared?" she asked. Their server appeared then and Mistress Evelyn ordered for them both without glancing at the menu. Again, his mind flashed to Keira.

"She doesn't know the extent...of all this," he said, once their server was gone.

"But clearly she's giving you what you need or you'd have come running back to The Club already."

She wasn't wrong. They'd been taking turns Topping and bottoming, kind of. He topped her and she sorted through various fantasies she had stored in her imagination. And Daniel followed through with those fantasies, no matter how ridiculous. The nights they'd spent at his place she'd been okay with, and then enthusiastic about him moving from bare hand spankings to the flogger. She didn't care much for the paddles. There was regular vanilla sex. Lots of that;

more than Daniel was used to, but he couldn't bring himself to mind. He felt himself getting hard thinking about it. Sometimes after a long day at work, retreating to her apartment and falling into her bed, just to make love to her, was the best part of his day.

"I don't think she's ready for The Club."

"Or you're not ready to bring her to The Club. Which is it?

"Possibly a little bit of both. How long before I'm banned?"

Daniel smiled again at Evelyn's laugh. He knew he sounded ridiculous, but he was only half joking. How long could he stay away, self-marooned on the Isle of Keira before his Friends-in-Kink stopped sending lifeboats? There had been texts from Marcos, calls from Meegan. Philip had even sent him an invite to a kink exposé in San Francisco at the start of the New Year. People had expectations of him. At some point he was going to have to show up.

"We would never ban you. Ever. We were hoping The Club would be yours one day, if you want me to be completely honest." Mistress Evelyn said the words so casually it made Daniel blink.

"I—excuse me?"

"You don't think Philip and I have talked about it?"

"Well I don't particularly like thinking about you two not being around for The Club *not* to be yours."

"It's going to happen one day, sweetheart. And even before then we'd like to retire from everything. Well, from the responsibility. We want to be around to see the place given into the right hands."

"But I couldn't even afford the space and everything else—"

"That's what the membership is for."

Daniel had almost forgotten. Membership to the club came with several caveats, one being that you paid a sum to be invited to one of the most exclusive bondage establishments on this side of the country, but Daniel had never paid a dime. Master Philip wouldn't let him.

"I'm flattered, but what about Meegan, or Shane, or the boys?" Wouldn't their sons want dibs on such a valuable piece of downtown LA real estate?

"Meegan's not right for it. Jordy and Ray have their trust. You don't think we're making the right decision?"

"No. I just…I don't know what to say."

"Say you'll think about it. Say you'll consider it a gift from us to you."

"And Keira? You want to know how serious I am about her? How she plays into all this?"

Evelyn frowned. "No. Why would you think that? I just want to know more about this girl who has you so wrapped up. Nothing beyond that."

"I'm sorry, I didn't mean to say that—"

"Sweetheart, if you're still working things out with her, take your time. Relationships develop and play out in the way they're meant to. No matter what happens, we're here for you, and Keira for that matter. If she needs us."

"Thank you. I appreciate that."

"Can you bring her to the Christmas party? It'll be more cookies and punch than kink anyway. She'll have a great time."

Daniel didn't doubt that for a minute, but still…

"Give me more news. How are things at the fireworks factory? How's Mama?"

The change of subject actually helped. Work and family Daniel could talk about with ease. He wasn't exactly sure what his problem was when it came to Keira and The Club, but he needed to figure it out.

Keira's glance flicked to the clock at the top of her computer screen. Daniel would be there any moment.

She was still sitting on her bed, forcing herself to breathe. Everything was going to be fine.

ItsKeiraTime: I'm going to chicken out.

LoriNLynn+Twins: don't you dare. you said he said he loved you. you've been hanging out AND sleeping together for weeks!

ItsKeiraTime: but it was a like a post sex buddy-buddy "i love you, buddy" kind of i love you.

LoriNLynn+Twins: whatever. guys dont accidentally say i love you. nobody does.

Keira wasn't exactly sure she believed that, considering Daniel hadn't said it again since that night at his place, but she knew there was something serious between them. They spent all their free time together and when they weren't together they were texting each other.

LoriNLynn+Twins: just ask him and if he says no then you know where you stand with him.

ItsKeiraTime: no you're right.

As Keira hit 'send', her doorbell rang.

ItsKeiraTime: he's here. gotta jet.

LoriNLynn+Twins: Good luck! Lynn says good luck too!

Keira sent two kissy faces and an XOXO before signing out of her email. Part of her plan included her laptop, but she didn't want chat boxes and alerts popping up while she was trying to focus. She set down her computer and went to the door. Daniel was there, looking all perfectly handsome and beautiful and hot. He'd just gotten a haircut, the sides of his head practically buzzed clean. Keira actually bit her lip as she looked at him. *God, please let him say yes.*

He held up the bag in his hand. "Chicken fried rice and just chicken fried rice."

"You kept asking what else I wanted. I just wanted the rice. But thank you. Come in."

He slid by her, kissing her forehead as he headed toward the couch. "You okay?" Was it that obvious? Her nerves were so twisted up she was practically vibrating.

"Yeah I'm fine," she said, even though her voice nearly cracked. She watched Daniel as he made himself comfortable and he watched her as she stood by the door like it wasn't her apartment, like they hadn't made plans that involved them actually being on the same side of the room.

"Actually, no. Well yeah. I wanted to ask you something."

"Okay…" He slowly eased back into the couch cushions, a look of dread clouding his face.

"Gosh, I should have just said 'Daniel, we need to talk.'"

"Yeah, that's how it sounds."

"It's not bad. I swear. Okay." Keira rushed over to the couch and made a space on the coffee table in front of him. "So tonight I had two plans, but one plan depends on what you say to the thing I have to ask you. Okay?"

"Okay, shoot."

"I really like you and I really like all the time we've been spending together and I love that you will watch *Galaxis* with me and cartoons, and all the other silly stuff I like. And you indulge my weirdly specific food requests. You're awesome. I like you. But I also know that we're kinda different. I'm more traditional, you could say, and I thought about it, being a hip woman, keeping up with the times who can be with someone and sleep with someone who's seeing other people, but I'm not really. Not that I think you're seeing other people. I don't know when you'd find the time, but yeah. I was wondering what you thought about possibly being exclusive. Like you being my boyfriend."

"You're asking me if I want to be your boyfriend?"

Keira wanted to throw up. "Yeah."

Daniel looked at her for a moment, his expression completely blank. The silence would be perfectly filled with the sound of her barfing. And it would be if he didn't say or do something soon.

"You can say no. I mean of course you know you can say no. But if you said no I would understand. I'm a weirdo fangirl sci-fi geek who talks too much. I'm not sure I'd want to date me either. I just thought I'd ask."

Daniel slid forward and took her hand. His fingers were so warm. She thought of how they felt trailing down her back as she fell asleep in his arms and she wondered if that was over. If he was soothing her one last time before he walked out of her life.

"You know you might be my first real girlfriend since high school?"

"Really?"

"Yup. You know me, living that wild bachelor life."

"Oh, I just figured… You're so hot though."

Daniel's laugh made Keira bite the inside of her lip again. "Well not quite as beautiful as you, but I'll take that as a compliment."

"Can I take the fact that you didn't just jump out my window as a sign that you're saying yes?"

"Yes, baby. I'm saying yes."

Keira let out a huge sigh, letting her whole body sag forward. But that was just the first part.

"What sort of plans for the evening come with a yes?" Daniel asked.

"Well, you can pick. One second."

Keira jumped up and ran to her room. She'd prepared everything she needed and put it into a Melrose Fitness tote for easy transport to the other end of her apartment. Daniel hadn't made a break for it while she was gone, confirming that the yes still stood.

"So there's a Twilight Zone marathon on tonight and I thought we could play a combination drinking/stripping game to the repetitive themes. Or… I was hoping you'd let me try that edging thing you told me about."

Daniel's eyebrow went up. "What's in the bag?"

Keira reached down and started pulling out the pieces of plan B. "I got this ball gag cause you said you wanted to be gagged. And then I was going to get handcuffs, but no—'cause, duh. I did some research and this rope was highly recommended. The store only had this length in neon green. I hope that's okay."

"Green's fine."

"Then I got this oil that shouldn't stain the couch or clothes, and then I got this. The man at the store said this was the best one, besides a full kit." She handed Daniel the box enema. When she looked up, his expression had gone from pleasantly surprised to pure shock.

"Is this too much? You can tell me if I'm doing it wrong. All the edging stuff I looked up seemed to be better for the guy if some prostate stimulation was involved. I got these cool black rubber gloves too. He said some people like them. They look sexy, I guess," she added with a shrug. They were pretty neat.

"No, this isn't too much at all. Why don't we throw on the Twilight Zone and then we'll put all this into play."

"Great. I did a lot of reading. I'm kinda aching to apply my knowledge."

"I bet you are. Come here," Daniel said as he slid even farther to the edge of the couch. Keira met him halfway, brushing her lips against his until he leaned in a little more. Then his arms were around her and they were both standing, lost in the kiss. She was so glad she hadn't chickened out. If she had, she wouldn't be the proud, new owner of this awesome boyfriend who also happened to be the best kisser on Earth. She couldn't wait to tell Lori.

Daniel took his time getting ready. Not that he wasn't familiar with this sort of preparation, but he needed a few moments to think. It wasn't a matter of what he had just done, what he'd just agreed to. Keira was great, she was perfect. Any man would be lucky to have her and she'd decided that she wanted him to be that man. And that was all well and good for tonight, but at some point he was going to have to make the tough call. He was going to have choose between Keira and The Club and these people he'd come to know as his family.

He hadn't seen anyone from his kinky life in weeks. There had been plenty of texts and calls, but after he got a message from Marcos saying that Mistress Evelyn had mentioned he was some seeing someone, a fact he confirmed, the texts and calls stopped. He knew they were being respectful and giving him space, but there was a sense on everyone's part, even his own, that he would be back. It was just a matter of time.

But now the decision had been made for him. Keira had said it out loud, plain and clear. She wanted him to herself. Daniel was pretty sure tag-teaming various submissives with Master Philip was out of the question. He could kiss his amateur porn-making days goodbye. And if he really wanted to see this relationship with Keira through, it would probably be a good idea to decline Mistress Evelyn's offer to take over The Club.

But he figured he could worry about all of that another time, at least after the weekend.

He finished up in the bathroom, stashing the towel he'd used after his shower in the hamper.

He could hear Keira talking to herself as he came down the hall.

"Gosh, I hope I don't screw this up. He needs his circulation."

Daniel was just about to ask what she was talking about when he turned the corner and saw what she was wearing. She stood as soon as she saw him, gripping the length of rope in her hand. She glanced down when she realized he wasn't staring at her face.

"Oh, I—ah—I figured I should wear something dominatrix-y, but this was all I could come up with."

Daniel looked her up and down, taking in the black push-up top that came with ribbons that she'd criss-crossed down her torso. There were black thigh-high socks with white stripes that added to the overall sexiness of the situation. What he couldn't take his eyes off of was the pair of lace panties she was wearing that appeared to be crotchless.

Daniel swallowed. "I think it'll work just fine. Turn around a sec."

"Um, excuse me. I think I'm in charge tonight."

"Just humor me."

"Fine." Keira spun around with a sigh, bending over a bit to give Daniel the view he was clearly looking for.

Definitely crotchless. Somehow he managed to keep his hand to himself, but his erection, which had started to rise during his preparations, now showed up for the full occasion. It was just as difficult to keep his hand off his dick.

"Good?" Keira asked, still slightly bent over.

"Yeah we're good."

"Excellent. Please come to the couch, but remain standing. Please."

Daniel followed orders, coming to stand in front of the couch, where Keira had put down a thick towel to cover the cushions. Her laptop was open on the coffee table. A video he'd watched a while ago, a rope tutorial by Madam May, an amazing bondage expert, was queued up.

"Also, excuse the laptop and the video. I want to make sure I get this right. Just bear with me."

"I'm bearing."

Daniel stood patiently as Keira began binding his arms to his sides. She talked to herself the entire time, but she barely glanced at the screen as the knots and loops came together down the length of his torso. He wondered how many times she's practiced. And on whom. After a few short moments she stood back to admire her work.

"Is it too tight?"

Daniel moved his arms, just a fraction of an inch. "Perfect."

"Great," she said with the enthusiasm he'd loved about her from day one. "Can you snap?"

Daniel responded with a loud snap of his fingers.

"Excellent."

He had to laugh at the huge smile on Keira's face and the way she bounced up on the balls of her feet, but she had every right to be proud of herself. This was a night of firsts for her and so far she was knocking every bit of it out of the park.

"Would you like me to sit?" he asked.

"Yes, please. I must administer the ball gag."

Daniel sat, shaking his head at her silliness. She carefully secured the gag in his mouth, then gave him a light shove. It wasn't enough to move him, but he still flopped back against the couch.

Keira slid onto the floor between his legs. "K, here I go. Snap if the pleasure is just too much for you."

All Daniel could do was nod.

He channeled years of training, years of patience, as he watched her grab the bottle of massage oil and proceed to pour the slick liquid all over his dick. He watched her face as she watched the warm liquid run down his balls. She added more, then wasted no time spreading it around his sac.

"This stuff is safe for me to swallow. Not saying that I'm going to be putting anything in my mouth, but just in case you wanted to know."

Daniel let out a rough breath through his nose, his sign that he understood.

Keira started on his balls, massaging them slowly. He thought about closing his eyes, shutting everything out so he could focus on the feel of Keira's hands and the sound of her voice, and not how badly he wanted to lay her out of the floor and fuck her senseless. But he had to watch her, to look at her beautiful face when she tilted her head to the side and gave his scrotum and ass a thorough inspection.

"Your skin is so soft. It's so weird how soft taint skin is."

Daniel snorted because this was his girlfriend now, his Keira, talking so matter-of-factly about the softness of his taint, and instead of turning him off it just made him want her more. He wouldn't change her ability to keep every moment they spent together light and full of humor for anything. He slid a little farther down on the couch and spread his legs a little wider.

Keira really started in on him then, using one hand to slowly stroke his cock while she massaged his balls. So slowly he knew it would be a breeze to hold off until she was ready for him to come. The only frustration came from not being able to touch her, not being able to kiss her. Those thoughts had him staring at her more carefully as she touched him. He started to memorize the features of her face, the way her straightened hair looked pulled back. Her lips.

She took him into her mouth after a while, talking to him and teasing him as she slurred up and down his shaft. She knew he wouldn't come and she knew he couldn't talk, but still she asked him how good it felt, if he wanted her to keep going. He groaned and grunted in the affirmative. Her tongue was enough to make him want to cover those, soft plump lips with his come.

The teasing didn't last forever though. She started sucking him in earnest, not for his pleasure, but for her own. Sitting up on her knees, she leaned over his lap and started going to town. For a moment, Daniel lost himself, actually let himself forget that he was supposed to be holding off. He snapped three times sharply. When Keira looked up he shook his head. Her lips were all slick and glossy.

"Do I need to stop? Are you close?"

He nodded with another grunt.

"Okay. I'll back off. This is easier than I thought." The wink she threw him was unnecessary. He was already coming to terms with how hard this was going to be. Daniel loved edging. He loved the tension it created all over his body, and the inevitable release that was always worth the wait, but he didn't want to wait. No. Not tonight. He wanted Keira, now. It was too soon though. He already agreed to her terms. Unless he wanted to end the scene altogether, he would just have to suck it up and wait 'til the moment where he could take her properly.

More oil then, along his shaft and all over his lap. She massaged his hips and his stomach before making her way down his thighs. The lack of direct stimulation helped a bit, but not for long because she was soon back on his cock, with her hand this time, while her other fingers started toying with his ass.

"Do you want the gloves?"

Daniel nodded. He'd already pictured her snapping the black latex into place. She paused long enough to do just that and Daniel's cock jumped at the sound.

One finger then two gently probed his ass. The intrusion was too much and still not enough. He was groaning and close to thrashing on the couch, but his hips were the only thing that moved; his hips and the heaving of his chest, until he snapped again. He was gonna come.

"You really like that don't you?" she asked, before she went at him with just her tongue. Her mouth was everywhere, licking and kissing and sucking. She asked him again and again if she was doing things right. More groans and grunts and pumping of his hips as her head turned this way and that.

She brought him to the edge again, taking turns between using her mouth and her hands, stroking his cock, and fucking his ass with her slender fingers. Daniel didn't expect her to be so good at this. He'd never enjoyed this so much, not with anyone else.

Keira stood up and tugged off the latex gloves.

"I'm sorry. I have to do something a little selfish."

As long as you keep touching me, you can be as selfish as you want. She did one better. She straddled his lap and sat on his dick.

He was already slick from the oil and her mouth, but her pussy was so wet and so warm, he could only squeeze his eyes shut to keep himself from ejaculating. It was his only way to claw at some sense of self-control. She felt too good. Daniel automatically thrust his hips up, burying himself as deep as she could take him. Keira cried out, falling forward to brace herself on his shoulders. He moved his hips again, pumping into her until she begged him to stop.

"Wait, wait. Hold on," she said, practically panting. "Just let me ride you."

Daniel groaned his disapproval, but gave in, settling in the couch so she could set the pace. He watched her as she got herself off, wishing she'd lose the strappy bra top so he could watch her nipples. It would have been even better if her nipples were in his mouth. He didn't care if this was her night. As soon as she untied him, he was taking over.

Keira came, slowing the vicious rocking of her pelvis long enough to draw out her orgasm. Daniel held off, focusing all his energy on not coming inside of her tight, throbbing pussy. But she didn't savor it, not the way he was hoping she would. She hopped off him, rubbing her clit as she retreated to the far end of the couch.

"Come," she said with a breathy sigh. Her fingers were still busy with their exploration. "Come now."

The only words Daniel's body wanted to hear. He gave in, letting all the sensations and built up frustration take control. Come shot out of his cock and up his chest in thick jets. Keira came back to him and started to tug off the gag. Jizz was still leaking from his swollen tip. He had two more nuts in him in, at least. She was in such deep shit once he got out of this rope.

As soon as the gag was off, she went for his stomach, licking up whatever she could find on his skin and in between the ropes. And then she kissed him.

"Go get the condoms out of my jacket," Daniel said when he had a moment to breathe and swallow the come she'd just put in his mouth. "And then I want you to untie me."

"But we're not done yet. You haven't pizza'd yet." Keira's attempt at arguing was cute, considering she was already reaching for his coat. She dropped the condoms on the coffee table and then made quick work of the ropes binding his arms.

"Is it bad that I set a timer?" she asked as she untangled the final knots.

"I wouldn't expect anything else from you. How'd we do?"

Keira glance at her computer then back at him with this toothy grin. "Two hours and twenty-three minutes. You think we can beat it next time?"

Daniel stood then pulled her closer, kissing her face. "I'm sure we can. Put a condom on me."

"You ready again?" she asked, even though she was already reaching for a rubber. He didn't even bother to answer because she was already sliding it over his cock. But he did ask her, "Are you worn out?"

"No," she replied, a hint of bashfulness coloring her voice. She wasn't used to being this greedy.

"We'll have to do something about that." Daniel kissed her once more. And then he turned her around and bent her over the couch.

CHAPTER SEVEN

Keira didn't know it was possible to smile for two days straight, but when she woke up Monday morning, way before the sun, she was still grinning like an idiot. Her first two clients even noticed she was perkier than usual, but she didn't think it would be professional to tell them that she had a new man. It would be extra unprofessional to go into the explicit details of how they spent their first weekend coupled up, but thinking about those explicit things just made her smile even more. Yeah, this kind of happy was something she could get used to.

When she came back to the gym with her lunch, Grant finally asked what had her on cloud eleven, even after she'd spent part of the morning in a one-on-one with her least favorite client.

Armando came into the office just as she was about to spill the beans. She figured she should tell them both.

"Well, Daniel and I are a couple now."

"Oh yeah?" Grant's face lit up with pleasant surprise. Armando, on the other hand… Keira tried not to be bothered by the look of horror spreading across his face. She did a double take before she turned her attention back to Grant.

"Yeah. I uh, I asked him if he wanted to go steady. You know, be exclusive 'cause I'm in high school and I need to define my commitment."

Grant shrugged that last bit off. "Nah. Violet asked me to be her boyfriend. Shit, it was good for me. I think it's fine to define a relationship when it gets to that point. And you guys have been hanging for what? Like a month?"

Thirty-three and a half days. "Yeah, something like that."

"Well, there you go. I'm happy for you guys."

"Thank you," Keira said and she meant it, but she was slightly distracted by the fact that Armando's eye looked like it was about to start twitching at any moment. "Are you okay?"

"Yeah. Yeah. I'm happy for you guys. I'll be right back." He turned on his sneakers and walked right out of the office.

"What is going on with him?" Keira asked.

Grant shrugged. "Who knows? So, I guess you'll be coming to the Christmas party at Master Phillip's."

"Oh, I don't know. Daniel hasn't mentioned it yet."

"I'm sure he will. It's this weekend. Violet had to keep reminding me."

"Oh. I'll be back." She didn't mean to be so dismissive, especially since Grant was being supportive, but she had to know what Armando's deal was.

Keira wandered back out to the gym and saw Armando through the frosted front doors, talking on his phone. She marched outside, catching him off guard.

"She *is* my business, man! She's my friend! I—" He cut himself off when he realized he wasn't alone.

"Are you talking to Daniel?"

Armando's face fell. "Ah—"

Keira held out her hand. "Let me talk to him."

"Uh…here."

Keira took the phone, but kept her eyes firmly on Armando. What the heck was going on? "Hey, it's me."

"Hey." Daniel did not sound happy.

"Is everything okay?"

"Yeah, Armando's just worried about you. He doesn't trust me."

"Is there a reason he shouldn't?" Keira asked around the sudden sour taste in her mouth.

"No, not at all. He's just paranoid because I'm a pervert and he thinks I'll corrupt you, but I think we both know it's a little late for that."

"Yeah, I think so," Keira replied. Her smile was back. "Oh, Grant said something about a Christmas party this weekend? Do I need a dress?"

"Uh, yeah. I completely forgot about that." Daniel was quiet for a second before he went on. "It's at the club, as in the bondage club. Are you sure you want to go?"

"Do I have to bondage with strangers?"

Daniel's laugh made it easier for her to ignore Armando while he stood there watching her. "No, you don't, babe. Unless you want to."

"I think I'm good. I have a client soon. Do you want to talk to Armando again?"

"No, I don't. I'll text you later, aight?"

"'Kay." Keira said her goodbyes then hit END on the screen. Then she turned on Armando. "What gives?"

"I've just never known Daniel to have a girlfriend. I don't want you to be the guinea pig, if it ends badly."

"That kinda sucks, Mando. I mean, that's a crappy thing to say," Keira said, despite the sudden tightness in her throat. "He's been great to me and I really like him. And *you* introduced us. I know you didn't think we would hook up, but isn't it better that we found each other?"

"I—No, you're right."

"You can have two single, unhappy friends, or two friends that are happy together."

"You're right, you're right. I'm sorry." Armando let out an uneasy laugh and then pulled Keira into his arms, a familiar hug they'd shared dozens of times. "You know how protective I am of my sisters."

"Well, I'm not one of your sisters and you're not the boss of me. Well actually you are, but you get what I mean." Keira stepped back and handed Armando his phone. He seemed to relax.

"You sound like Daniel. He basically said the same thing."

"Good. Stop being bossy and just be happy for us."

"Alright, alright. Let's get back in here. I've got a client soon. And your lunch is probably getting cold."

Keira followed Armando inside. She appreciated that he cared about her so much, but everything with Daniel was going to be fine. Better than fine. Great.

★

During another meeting about the Super Bowl, Daniel decided the Christmas party would be the last function he attended at The Club. If he wanted to be with Keira, he couldn't share his life with all these other people who thought he was nothing but his kinks. He didn't know how he was going to break the news to Miss Evelyn, or Philip, but he would think of something. After the party.

Keira reached over and took Daniel's arm. He looked so sexy in his dress shirt and perfectly tailored vest. They were on their way to a party. A fancy, kinkified Christmas party with Daniel's fancy, kinky friends. And Grant and Armando. They were fancy too, but Keira was interested in meeting the rest of these mysterious people Daniel rarely mentioned. He said something about his mentors owning the place, the way he described them seemed way too clinical to be the truth. You own a freaking kinky club? You have to be an interesting character. Keira couldn't wait to meet them and the rest of the people they deemed worthy to include on the guest list.

Still, Keira's excitement wasn't enough to distract from the fact that Daniel was acting really strange.

He'd been oddly distant the last few days. He told her he was fine a bunch of times, but Keira was picking up all kinds of not-fine vibes. Daniel was an honest man, and pretty straightforward. If something was bugging him she just had to trust he would tell her when he was ready.

"So when the party's over, your place or mine?" Keira asked, code for 'do you want top me tonight or not?'.

Daniel glanced over at her, a small smile finally touching his lips. "We'll go to my place. I think it's finally time we tie you up properly with some rope."

Keira's pussy clenched at the thought. She liked when he bound her with the bondage tape, but the rope would be fun.

Daniel pulled his SUV down an alley between two warehouses to where a valet stand and velvet rope had been set up at the door. Daniel handed off his key and helped Keira out of the car.

"Is it okay for me to be nervous?" she asked, as she took his hand.

"There's nothing to be nervous about. Come on." They took a short hall to a freight elevator that took them down one floor. It opened to a small receiving area where a bouncer sat on a stool. The short white guy lit up when he saw Daniel.

"Hey man! Where have you been? It's been weeks." They did that dude hug thing with the slap on the back.

"Just been busy."

"We thought we'd lost you." As the bouncer spoke he glanced at Keira in a peculiar way. Half way between curious and annoyed. She tried not to frown when he introduced himself as Trent, the club security.

Trent opened the door for them and Daniel led her inside. The party was already in full swing, people and things filling up the massive space. Christmas music was playing over the sound system and there were Christmas decorations up everywhere. Some people were dressed in regular party attire, like Daniel and herself, but there were a fair bit of people in leather bondage gear, accented with Santa hats of course. Daniel leaned toward her and pointed to a large window that ran along the wall about twenty feet above their heads. It was tinted so you couldn't see through. "Mast— Philip and Evelyn use the top floor as a home away from home and this functions as the club proper."

Keira just nodded, her anxiousness overtaken by sheer curiosity and shock. She looked at the various contraptions around the room. A set of medieval stocks, this large wooden X thing, a giant bird cage that looked big enough to hold three people. There was a stage and two smaller stages with stripper poles. Small tables with chairs filled the middle of the floor, but each little nook and cranny that ran along the outer walls housed a different device and a perfectly positioned leather couch or love seat, for spectators Keira assumed. Nothing was being used though. Everyone was just milling about the space, socializing. There was more, Keira could see as she looked around, but Daniel veered her over to the bar area where Violet and Nailah were standing. They were fully dressed.

"Where are your boys?" Daniel asked as he and Keira hugged them both hello.

Nailah rolled her eyes and pointed up toward the window. "They got recruited to be Santa's elves."

"Is it okay if you hang with the ladies for a moment? I have to go talk to Philip." Daniel asked Keira. Maybe it had to do with whatever was bugging him.

"Yeah, sure."

"We'll take care of her," Violet said with a smile.

Daniel kissed her on the cheek. "I'll be right back."

"Yeah," Keira said. She hoped their talk fixed things.

"Everything okay?" Violet asked when he took off across the room.

"Don't worry," Nailah said. "Armando ditched me the first time we came here too. It's like they don't know how to act when their worlds collide." Maybe she was onto something.

"Yeah, things are cool. I think. I think he's just having a bad day."

"Well just hang with us."

"Yeah, he'll be back."

Keira ordered herself a soda and stood by as Nailah and Violet tried to give her the skinny on the people in their line of sight. People they didn't know, Nailah started making up mean, gossipy stories about. Keira tried not to laugh, but Nailah had a way with words.

Soon a tall, younger-looking white girl came over to them and offered them raffle tickets. She had on a set of felt reindeer ears and not much else beyond the red paint on the tip of her nose. A red leather body harness wove its way down her torso, but it did nothing to cover her nipples or the glossy slit between her legs. Whoever had dressed her had gotten her nice and wound up. Looking at her made Keira even more excited to get back to Daniel's place.

The girl handed her a ticket. "What are these for?" Keira asked.

"For when Santa arrives," the girl said cheerfully.

"Meegan, this Daniel's girlfriend, Keira." The second Nailah made the introduction, Meegan's expression dropped, shock then pain hitting her eyes. "Keira, Meegan belongs to Master Philip and Mistress Evelyn."

Meegan swallowed, her eyes darting to the floor. "If you'll excuse me." She bolted to the next group of people and kept handing out tickets, looking like she was fighting the urge to cry.

"What the heck was that all about?" Keira asked.

Violet glanced at Nailah, but, being less coy and tactful, Nailah just spit out the truth. "Meegan has the hots for Daniel. She probably didn't think he'd show up with a date, let alone a girlfriend."

"But if she belongs to—"

"It's not like that. Philip and Evelyn are married. They own Meegan as a pet and a plaything. She's not allowed to be dominated by anyone but them, but she can date other submissives. I mean get it, but you'd think Daniel would have asked her out by now if he was interested."

"Nailah, Jesus."

A strange kind of heat flashed over Keira's body and her stomach started to flip. She looked over to see Violet rubbing her face, annoyed.

"I'm sorry," Nailah said. "I'm working on not being so insensitive. Daniel's here with you. That's what matters."

Keira had no idea why she was so upset, other than the fact that she hated confrontation. Nailah was right. Daniel was here with her. Daniel was *her* boyfriend, but why did this Meegan girl seemed so shocked to hear it, especially if she and Daniel were any kind of close? Maybe he hadn't told her yet. Or maybe he wasn't planning to tell her anything.

Violet handed Keira a small bottle of ice water. The large gulp she took only made her feel a little better because, really, Daniel wasn't with her. She couldn't see him anywhere.

✳

Daniel headed back down to the floor just as conflicted as before. For someone so determined to make up his mind, he was getting nowhere. He loved Keira and he wanted to be with her for the long haul, but he needed The Club and his kink community too.

They were a part of his life and such an integral part of who he had become as a man, and a switch.

He'd had an interesting talk with Master Philip. Grant and Armando, who had been in the room and done their best to listen and not comment, only added that whatever he decided to do, he better not hurt Keira in the process. That right there was the tricky part. If he took over The Club someday, he would want Keira by his side. If she was by his side, he was going to marry her. If they planned to see this through, if he finally got up the guts to propose to her, she had to become a member of the club. But he had no idea how to approach her about peer counseling and proper training. He had to make her see that he could be involved and still be faithful to her.

Daniel found Keira right where he'd left her, at the bar chatting with the girls.

"How's it going?" he asked, as he pulled Keira into his arms. It didn't go unnoticed that she was a little stiff.

"Had a pleasant run-in with Meegan," Nailah said, giving him a look that said there was a sixty percent chance he'd be going home alone tonight. Just then Anthony, a Dominant he'd played with numerous times, came over to say hello. Everything was going fine until…

"All this time you've been away, I hope you and Keira have at least made some new clips. Your adoring public is waiting for new material." A statement innocent enough, but… "Actually I was hoping you'd recreate the one you made with Pamela. You know, we talked about the quality and the angles. Keira would be perfect for that."

Daniel tried to ignore the fact that Anthony glanced at the roundness of Keira's ass as he made the comment. "No, you're right, but we haven't gotten around to that yet."

"Oh that's a shame. Keira, I'm sure you've seen Daniel's handiwork. You have a favourite video yet?"

She looked over her shoulder at him, so much subtle murder in her eyes. "Um, I'm not sure I've seen them all." She hadn't seen any.

"We made some good ones, didn't we, Dan?" Anthony meant well, but he needed to shut up. Luckily the sound of sleigh bells signified the start of the festivities. Anthony excused himself and found a seat.

Daniel pulled Keira closer and whispered in her ear. "I promise I'll explain later."

"I bet."

Master Philip entered and took center stage with Grant and Armando at his side, each with sacks of unwrapped kink toys to be raffled off and exchanged. Daniel usually put himself into the raffle, but this year he put in a gift certificate for an erotic massage. The effort was lackluster at best, but no one would know it was from him. That was the point.

Things kicked off all in good fun. Keira's number was called third and she went to the front of the room to claim a pair furry handcuffs and edible panties from Grant. They shared a good laugh and some words Daniel couldn't make out from across the room.

"These are both for you to wear," Keira said when she made her way back to the bar.

He took the box of panties out of her hand. "That means you're going to have to eat them." He laughed when Keira turned up her nose, and with good reason. He'd eaten those thin pieces of flavored plastic before. Keira stepped back into his arms and continued fiddling with the furry cuffs as they watched the rest of the ridiculous spectacle.

When Keira settled against his chest, laughing, asking questions, sharing appropriately snarky comments with Violet and Nailah, he figured whatever had happened with Meegan and the awkwardness with Anthony had been forgotten or, at least, tabled for a calm, rational discussion. Yeah everything was going just fine, until Marcos went up to the stage. Just fine, even as Armando handed Marcos a heavy-duty leather flogger. Just fine, even as Marcos turned around and started scanning the room. Just fine, until his gaze fell on Daniel.

"I'm accepting this gift under one condition," Marcos called out.

"And what is that, little boy?" Philip replied in his best Santa voice.

"I want Daniel Song to flog me with it tonight. He hasn't been here in over a month and I think he owes me a little something, plus owing you fine people a show."

To Daniel's expected horror, several people around the room joined in with similar complaints and jabs about his absence. He did his best to laugh all their comments off.

"I'm sorry, Marcos. Not tonight," he called back.

"Oh come on. I'm sure Keira will let you play with us. Come on." And that's where shit really went south.

"Oh, so she's your Mistress now?" Meegan said, loud enough for everyone in the whole place to hear.

Meegan was quickly admonished by a sharp look from Mistress Evelyn, but the damage was done.

Keira looked up at him. "You can play with whoever you want. Really, I don't care."

She didn't mean it, not by a long shot. It was written all over her face, but then was not the time or the place to discuss the real issue at hand.

Daniel tried to play it cool. "I don't think so. Maybe one of Santa's elves wants to help you out."

"Um no. *I* don't think so." Everyone laughed at Nailah's outraged rebuttal. She'd staked clear monogamous claim on Armando the moment she'd joined the club.

"Don't worry, my little Marcos. Santa and Mrs. Claus will treat you to something special before we tuck you in," Mistress Evelyn said, finally ending the debate.

Marcos jumped off the stage with a "Yippee!" bringing the focus back to the front of the room and away from Daniel. And Keira. She was tense in his arms again. He knew he had to talk to her, but he didn't know where to start, which fuck up to try to fix first.

The night went on, more gifts, more absurdity. A performance or two. Daniel continued to introduce Keira around with mixed results. Some, like his good friend Anna and her submissive Caitlin, were kind and gracious, welcoming her to The Club, and others teased her as the wet blanket, keeping Daniel away from them for too long. Keira took it in stride, but Daniel could tell she was growing more and more uncomfortable. He asked her twice if she wanted to leave, but each time she said no, that she was having fun.

Near midnight, Daniel was ready to go. He made his rounds saying his goodbyes and explaining himself in as few words as possible. He was just another member for Christ's sake, but he was being treated like some sort of prodigal, as if The Club had stopped functioning in his absence, which he knew was far from the truth. He finally made his way back to Keira as Armando was handing her and Nailah their coats.

He took Keira's and helped her into it. Then she turned to him, fluffing out her hair. "I'm actually going to get a ride with Armando and Nailah. You stay. Hang out some more." The smile she flashed him was sour as hell.

Daniel glanced up at Armando, who met his gaze with the same type of look. Annoyed. Completely unimpressed. A little pissed. If Daniel wanted to stop Keira leaving with Armando and Nailah, he would have to go through Armando. This was not the time or the place.

"At least let me walk you out."

"Really, you don't—"

"Daniel. Let it go," Armando said.

Keira stepped between them and put her hand on Daniel's chest. Her touch did something to him. He wanted to pull her close, and please her for as long as she would let him, but that look was still in her eyes. She was leaving without him. "We'll talk later."

Knowing there was nothing else he could do, Daniel watched Keira walk out of The Club. He just hoped, with everything that had happened during this awkward as shit night, Keira wasn't walking out of his life.

CHAPTER EIGHT

Keira could hear Armando yelling when she came into the gym. She realized what or who he was talking about when he said a certain someone's name.

"Fucking Daniel, man. I don't know what the fuck he was thinking. I told him to take it easy with her. I told him the club wasn't her scene and then he brings her in there totally unprepared."

She couldn't make out what Grant said in response, but she could hear the muffled tone of his voice.

She walked right into the office, not wanting herself or her non-relationship with a certain someone to be topic of conversation for another minute. They both looked up when she came around the corner.

"Morning boys." She almost sounded cheerful, but the anger still radiating off Armando and Grant's hang-dog expression ruined any chance of her work day starting off on a light note. She'd already cried all weekend. Paced and cried and put away laundry in a huff and complained to Lori on chat. She'd spent more than enough time being upset about what had happened at the party. But Grant and Armando seemed to be just warming up.

"How you doing, Keir?" Armando said.

"Ugh, I'm fine." Keira tossed her bag on the floor and sank against the door jam.

"You talk to your boy?" Grant asked.

"No. He's been calling and stuff, but I only texted him back to let him know I didn't want to talk."

"Keira, listen. This is my fault. You told me you weren't into BDSM, and I know I didn't set you guys up, but I *know* Daniel. I put you in the mix with someone real fucking deep in the game. I knew better. We both did." She looked from Armando to Grant, who nodded in agreement.

Keira swallowed as the tears rose in her eyes. This was exactly what she didn't want. She already felt like an idiot, like an imposter who thought they could waltz right into their world of kinky fun and just adapt. She didn't need Grant and Armando to tell her that it was obvious to them too, obvious that she had no business at the club that night and even more obvious that she had no business being with Daniel.

"I'll be back." She went right to the ladies' locker room and sat down against the concrete wall. Daniel was at work, but she knew he would answer her texts. He always did.

I'm really mad at you.

Not even ten seconds went by before her phone chimed.

I know. I'm sorry.

Seriously. what was that all about?

I can't explain it over text.

I don't know if I want to see you. You made me feel so weird. Keira's throat tightened even more as she hit send.

Weird how? I'm so sorry.

Weird like an idiot.

Can I please come see you tonight?
I have more than a lot of explaining to do.
I understand if you don't want to be with me anymore.
Just want to talk to you.

That was the problem. Keira didn't know what she wanted. The Daniel she'd gotten to know, she was falling in love with. Actually, she was already there. And that's why his behavior the night of the party and everyone's reaction to him, to them, made her feel so uncomfortable.

Who the heck was this other Daniel and why had he hidden what seemed to be such an important part of himself from her? She had questions for sure, and she wanted answers, face to face. She was just terrified of which version of Daniel was going to show up. The last thing she wanted to was to be sweet talked into forgiving and then falling completely in love with a man who was okay with making her look like a fool.

Her fingers flew across her screen and she hit send without thinking.

Are you fucking that Meegan chick?

NO.
I haven't been with anyone since we met.

That didn't exactly make her feel better, but she needed to get the question off her chest. Meegan looked like she wanted to kill Keira the moment she found out who she'd shown up with. There was more than jealousy in her eyes. There was possession, and Keira did not sign up for a catfight.

Come over at 8 and don't think we're not going to talk about those videos that guy mentioned.

I'll tell you everything. I promise.

Great, Kiera thought. But was *everything* something she wanted to know?

✳

Daniel closed his eyes as he heard Keira undoing the lock to her front door. This was his chance. His one chance to unfuck the mess his personal life had become. He had one chance to tell Keira the whole truth, because he knew she didn't deserve anything less. She wouldn't stand for it. They wouldn't make it as a couple without it.

He tried not to smile when she opened the door. She was standing there in those microscopic shorts, and a *Galaxis* hoodie. Her hair was up and she had no make-up on, but her toenails were painted black. He'd painted them red for her the day of the party. The last time he'd seen her. She looked just as beautiful and adorable as ever. Daniel wanted to pull her into his arms or fall on his knees at her feet, but the look on her face suggested both would be a dumb-assed idea. Her eyebrows were drawn so tight together it looked like her anger and frustration with him was giving her a headache.

Daniel cleared his throat. "Keira."

"You can come in, but you are not staying."

"That's fair."

"I know it is. Come in."

Daniel followed her to the living room and sat beside her on the couch.

"No. Sit over there." She pointed to the armchair on the other side of the room. He made the mistake of laughing as he went to his assigned seat. "Don't want to be near me?"

"This isn't funny. I don't like the way you're making me feel right now and I don't want to be fooled into thinking this is all okay if you touch me."

"Fair enough."

"So, what the heck is your deal? I knew you were acting strange before we went to the party, but I still don't get what happened. Half the people in that room, actually everyone in that room, seemed to see me as some sort of enormous cock block. Which I guess I was, considering I'm or was kinda your girlfriend. But I want to know what you told them?"

His one chance.

"I didn't tell them anything and that was part of the problem. The other part was that I didn't tell you anything either. I lied to you, Keira."

She swallowed and pulled her legs up to her chest. "About how many things?"

"A few, but a few is too many. Especially when I take into account how I feel about you and how I hope you feel about me. I'm not Grant and I'm not Armando."

"I know that."

"I know you do, baby. Sorry. Keira. But when we met I think you thought in a lot of ways I was just like them. Grant and Armando are proper Dominants and the three of us belong to the same club and we run with the same crowd, but I'm part of what is called a Family. Grant and Armando aren't involved in this."

She seemed to be following so he kept going.

"Master Philip and Mistress Evelyn trained me in all things BDSM, but when my training was done they stayed a major part of my life and my sex life. Meegan is also a part of that family. As is Marcos."

"And you've had sex with all of these people?"

"Yes, I have, with the exception of Master Philip. But I have submitted to him. How do you feel about that?"

"I don't—I don't mind. I just wish you'd told me. I basically went into a room with all of these people you're involved with and you never told me. Can you imagine if I'd invited you to a party with all my exes or people I was still with, let them say all this stuff to you, but didn't explain it at all?"

"I'd be pissed. Like you are now. But you see how this makes me different from your boys?"

"Yes, I do. So what does this mean? Philip and Evelyn own you and you were just taking a break with me? Grant and Armando are free to date, but you have to go back to your family?"

"And that was where I started to fuck up."

"What?"

"That's what I thought—that I had to choose between you and the Family. I owe them my life, Master Philip and Mistress Evelyn. After my accident they were there for me in ways I can't even explain to you, Keira. I love them."

"Okay."

"When I met you I had no idea what was going to happen. I didn't even think about what Armando was asking me to do. It was a favor. A simple favor. Meet up with his friend for an afternoon, but…"

"But what?"

"But you. Do you have any idea how amazing you are? How bright and sunny and wonderful and smart? And you're an absolute freak even though you refuse to use swear words, which I think is the cutest shit ever.

"I didn't think I'd fall for you like this, but I did. But you only wanted part of me. You didn't want what Armando and Grant were into. I definitely didn't think you wanted The Club or this community we belong to, so I gave you what I could, on your terms, so I didn't scare you off."

"So it's my fault?"

"No. I could have walked away, but I didn't."

"And you lied to me?"

"I did, and other people I care about. I couldn't keep it up though. Philip and Evelyn want to give The Club to me when they're ready to retire. I would be the head of my own Family and the owner of The Club and I realized then that there was no way I could do that without you, so I went to Philip to ask him how to fix things between us and what I should say when I finally got up the nerve to propose to—"

"What?!" Keira sprang up right on the couch. "You were gonna ask me to marry you?! What the heck? Do it! Do it now!"

Her enthusiasm changed the whole climate of the room. Daniel practically snorted when he tried to hide his smile, but he wasn't finished. "I can't, because you don't know everything. You only know one part of me. After we started hanging out, I started to feel like—I thought a lot of people were using me at The Club. They love to see me perform, put on a show, and I was okay with that, until I met you. With you I started to see that something was missing. I thought kink and companionship were all I needed, but that's not true. I needed love, someone to be in love with. Someone to be in love with me."

Daniel pulled the flash drive out of his pocket and moved back over to the couch. Keira took the drive from his fingers when he offered it to her.

"That's everything I have. Every video I made. This will give you an idea of what you're really dealing with, with me. If you can watch this and still be with me then…"

"Then we'll get married and run a sex club and be swingers with Marcos and Meegan, and Grant and Armando and Nailah and Violet will come by and watch sometimes."

Daniel shook his head. "It doesn't have to be that. But it has to be something."

Keira chewed the inside of her lip for a moment as she rotated the drive in her hand. "Is there an expiration date on this? You're giving me a lot to think about."

"No expiration date." Daniel meant it. He wanted to be with Keira. He would wait.

"Okay. Well, you should go."

Daniel didn't want to push things, so he headed for the door. Keira followed so she could lock up behind him. He turned to her one last time.

"And the proposal? That's what Meegan was mad about. I've been single for over ten years. She knew if I started seeing someone it would be serious. She thought when I made the move it would be to her, but it wasn't. You're my queen, Keira. My princess. Only you."

"Okay, you have to leave." Keira shoved him out the door and slammed it in his face. But she was almost smiling when she did it.

"I love you," Daniel said through the door.

"Bye," Keira shouted back.

"I love you!"

"Go home!"

Enough was enough. Daniel walked out to his car, thinking maybe the two of them had a chance.

✳

Keira plugged the drive into her computer, but it took her forever to actually slide that little arrow over the first video. She watched the clip through fifteen minutes of a younger Daniel with Mistress Evelyn and another young man. It was interesting. Interesting enough for her to click the next and the next.

A couple hours later, when she finally had to take a break, two things were obvious. One, Keira was really wet and she was definitely going to have to masturbate. And the other surprised her a little. She'd seen Daniel in almost a dozen clips of different lengths, with almost two dozen people, and it didn't bother her. The opposite. It turned her on. He was right, they'd only scratched the surface of what they could do sexually, what Daniel was capable of doing with his various toys. And what he was capable of having done to him. Instead of making her want to take the drive and flush it down the toilet, or call Daniel and tell him to never contact her again, what Keira had seen had made her want to act.

She had to say something, do something, but she wasn't ready to talk to Daniel yet. Something she couldn't quite name had to be done first. She decided to sleep on it, think on it some more. Maybe she'd even confide in Armando and Nailah. He always looked out for her and Nailah always gave it to her straight. She watched a few more clips, ya know, just to be sure, then headed to bed with her vibrator.

In the morning Keira realized that she needed to figure out exactly what she wanted, and if she wanted all the details on Daniel and his kink crew, the person she really needed to speak with was Mistress Evelyn.

CHAPTER NINE

"Crap. Crapcrapcrapcrapcrap." Keira wasn't even close to being ready, but Daniel was on his way up to her apartment. She'd given herself plenty of time, but a new video of the cast of *Galaxis* went up online right as she got out of the shower. The panel was only an hour, but then Selia did a bunch of interviews with JD. They were so funny together. There was also a little bit in the b-roll where she saw herself in her Princess Orora costume. She had to roll that part of the video back ten or fifteen times.

Then she remembered that she had to be over at the Baker's for a little New Year's Eve dinner. The festivities at the club wouldn't kick off until ten. It was so kind of Evelyn to include her at their small dinner party. Keira didn't want to be late.

She'd actually gotten pretty close with Evelyn in the last couple of weeks. She liked Philip too, but she and Evelyn really clicked.

With a little help from Armando, she'd met up with Evelyn for brunch. Evelyn told her all sorts of stories about how she'd met Philip and the way they'd started and grown The Club and their Family. She'd also shared her unique perspective in being a black woman in the BDSM community. After, they'd had a pretty serious heart-to-heart about Daniel and all his bonehead moves. And then they'd talked at length about what Keira wanted, what she needed and what scared the crap out of her. They continued to talk on the phone and over text and planned to meet up again soon. No matter what happened with Daniel, Keira definitely felt like she'd made a great friend. Evelyn was awesome.

So yeah, Keira did not want to be late.

With her hair only a quarter straightened, Keira flung the door open just as Daniel rang the bell. She tried to ignore how good he looked in his tailored slacks and suit jacket. He had a simple white t-shirt on underneath, but he still looked delicious. Keira put her eyes back into her head.

"Thanks for agreeing to see me again."

"I'm late as crap. Come into the bathroom and we'll talk while I finish getting ready."

"Okay."

She talked as they walked. "Have you talked to Evelyn lately?"

"Yeah we talked this morning," he said hesitantly. "Why?"

"No reason. We've just been talking a lot lately."

"I see."

"Sit on the toilet. Tub's still wet."

Keira bit the inside of her lip when he did as she suggested. This gorgeous six-foot Korean man sitting on her closed toilet seat. In a suit. She grabbed her flat iron and went back to work.

"We talked about you a little."

"Oh?"

"Yup, and the club and stuff. She's a great lady."

"She is. What else did you two talk about?"

"Well, I told her about some of my misconceptions about BDSM and she cleared a lot of stuff up. Which was good. She also got Meegan to apologize to me. Meegan and I had a good talk too." Even if Keira could tell that the girl was still kind of bitter.

"You've done a lot of talking lately. Talking's good."

"Yup and she explained to me that you can be a part of their kink family and still be collared by someone outside of the family or someone who's planning to join."

Keira glanced at Daniel. He was squinting at her, confused as all get out. He also looked like he was turning a little red.

"She told me I could be any kind of Mistress that I want to be. That I don't ever have to wear leather. And she said I don't have to be mean or cruel. I can just be me. But she did say that I should go through some training so I understand how to treat all submissives the right way. I have to learn more about limits and negotiations and also what I need for the dominant part of myself and the submissive side. I thought that sounded pretty cool. Right?"

"All very cool. What else did you talk about?"

"Hold on. Crap. I hate doing the back." Keira sucked her nearly singed fingertip before she went on.

"We talked about you some more. I told her how I went out of my way to be myself with you. That so many guys didn't want the real me and after all that it was *you* who was holding back."

"Yeah? I fucked that up."

"But we figured that out, talked about why and what—"

"And what I need to do to get you back?"

"More like what you need to do to keep me."

Daniel swallowed, running his fingers through his hair. "Can I have the details?"

"Well, for one, you have to understand that I'm not Evelyn or Philip. I'm me and I like that. So I can't change to emulate what they are to you."

"I wouldn't want you to do that."

"I didn't think so, but I had to say it."

"Okay. What else?"

"Say you're sorry one more time."

"I'm sorry, love." Keira didn't move when he reached over and rubbed the bit of bare skin on her back. "I'll never lie to you again."

"You promise?"

"I promise." When he stood up Keira let him kiss her, but he wasn't completely off the hook yet.

"Good. Sit."

He obeyed immediately, dropping back down onto the toilet seat. "So what's the occasion tonight? Are you coming to the club later?"

"After dinner at the Bakers."

"Oh yeah?"

"Yup. You're my plus one."

"Am I?"

"Yup."

"Does this mean we're dating again?"

"Possibly."

"Then I have to do something first."

Keira froze when Daniel took the flat iron out of her hand and placed it on the counter. She stayed frozen in that same spot as he pulled a little ring box out of his pocket and showed her the sparkling ring inside. She let him slip it onto her finger. What other choice did she have?

Keira glanced up into Daniel's deep brown eyes before she looked back down at the aquamarine stone surrounded by diamonds. An embarrassing snort came out of her mouth.

"What, you don't like it?"

"No, no. I love it. I just—I'm just thinking about this AU fic I wrote and Orora totally gets an engagement ring like this."

"I asked Selia what ring would suit Orora best and she suggested this."

"Oh my god. That is so cool. Selia picked out my freaking ring. Lori is going to die."

"I thought a super fan like you would enjoy that." Daniel leaned down and kissed her again. "Should I still ask? I will if you want me to."

Keira shook her head. "No. We should probably meet each other's parents at some point, though, that kind of stuff, but you don't need to ask. And you already know my answer. Evelyn told me she and Philip got engaged after two weeks of knowing each other."

"We've known each other for over six weeks. We're practically ready for grandkids."

"True."

"When you know, you know."

"I agree."

"Do you need help getting ready?"

"Nope, but you can keep me company while I finish my hair."

"Done."

Keira watched Daniel out of the corner of her eye as he sat back on the toilet and made himself comfortable. This was her man alright, she thought, as she held in another snort. And it was somewhat of a relief. She'd never have to go on another bad first date again.

CHAPTER TEN

Keira slipped off her shoes and flopped onto her couch. Daniel didn't waste any time removing his prosthesis and getting undressed. It was her night to Top, but she needed a few minutes to get the stars out of her eyes. Daniel had taken her to an honest to goodness Golden Globes party. *Galaxis* wasn't up for anything, but JD was invited to a bunch of parties and asked Keira and Daniel if they wanted to tag along. They'd made it till one a.m. when JD subtly hinted that he was trying to take off with his own date. Keira didn't blame him. She was perfectly tipsy on champagne and she couldn't wait to get Daniel home and naked. Booze and fangirling made her extra horny.

"Would it be weird if I hung pictures of me and Selia around the apartment?" They'd taken about twenty of Keira showing her favorite actress the perfect ring she'd helped Daniel pick out.

"I don't think it would be weird at all, but they'll only be hanging up for another few months."

He had a point. In few months her lease would be up and she'd be moving to his house in Atwater

Village. They weren't getting married for another year, but the planning had begun. His mother's schedule at the casino was wonky so Keira, her mother, and Ms. Song had started discussing details over the phone. Daniel's mother was amazing. Loud and funny, but so sweet. It was like JD and Daniel had each taken the best parts of her. Keira would be proud to call her mom-in-law. Next month they were all flying up to meet her in person. Keira's parents had already met Daniel and they loved him, just like she knew they would.

A year from now they'd be joining their families at a small vineyard up north. And until then…

Daniel sank to the floor between her feet and rested his hand and his healed arm on his thighs.

Keira leaned forward and stroked his hair. "You want to record this?"

"Yes, my Princess."

Keira smiled. Princess was what she asked him to call her. She liked it better than Mistress.

"Go get my laptop then. And grab the lube and one of the dildos from my closet."

"Yes, Princess."

"Good boy."

When he came back they'd do the best to make a mess out of the little black dress she still wore and then off to bed. She made him lean down before she ordered him across her lap. She gripped his chin and kissed him.

"You're gonna come all over my lap and then you're going to lick it up. You'll enjoy that won't you?"

"Yes, Princess. You know I will."

"Good." Keira gave his ass a good slap before she sat back and guided him into position. When he was settled, she reached for the laptop and hit record. Keira couldn't wait for them to watch the playback, together.

THE END

But wait! There's more!

Turn the page for a little something extra
from
Grant and Violet...

BLESSED

(FIT #3.5)

"Luuuuucy! I'm home!"

Violet looked up from her tablet as her boyfriend/Dominant bounded through the door, his arms loaded with bags. She didn't exactly look at him, she glared. She was not in the mood for Grant's cheery bullshit. Christmas was two days away, but the Christmas spirit had been sucked right out of her.

She'd broken her ankle in the stupidest way, dancing on the stairs at her latest wrap party. Producing *Chef Masters* had been an absolute nightmare. So many divas, so many problems, little and huge, but it was the holidays. They'd wrapped under budget and her boss had suggested they throw a huge party for all the crew and production staff that had worked for them throughout the year. It was Violet's time to cut loose.

In line with her plan to drop some weight, she'd cut back significantly on her junk food and alcohol intake. She'd lost a few pounds and turned herself into a lightweight who could barely handle more than two drinks. Another thing she hadn't planned on? Landing herself a new man in the form of her personal trainer.

Things had changed a lot between them in the last eight months, professionally and personally. Grant still trained her, free of charge of course, but their relationship had grown intense. He introduced her to his kinks and the world of BDSM, shown her a true submissive side of herself that had been laying dormant, waiting for the right man to tap into her needs and wants. She loved Grant with all her heart as her boyfriend and Dominant and that's why she was so bummed when he couldn't make it to her wrap party. He had to fly home to help his parents with something that turned out to be minor. But Violet still sulked and drank herself stupid. So stupid she danced herself right off a flight of stairs and broke her ankle. A girl her size had no business walking in heels that high and definitely no business dancing in them like a drunken burlesque girl.

She'd planned to spend Christmas in Los Angeles with Grant instead of back home in Connecticut with her family. What she didn't plan for was spending her whole hiatus in Grant's condo with her leg in cast.

Poor Grant was trying his best though. He went out and bought a huge tree. Decorated seventy percent of it by himself when Violet got tired of standing with her crutches. Every morning when she woke up she found a couple more presents under said tree, meaning he'd wrapped them while she'd been asleep and just the idea of that made her want to cry, it was so cute.

He'd even gotten festive collars for his dog, Max and his cat, Bill. Whenever the TV wasn't on, Christmas music was playing through his surround system. He actually had pretty thorough and varied collection, but Violet couldn't find herself in the Christmas mood. She had something to tell Grant. Something she'd discovered while she was being tended to in the ER. Only her best friend Faye knew, but she had to tell him soon.

Grant dumped the bags on the counter and the floor then stood in all his Scandinavian god glory and smiled at her. "Don't you all get up at once."

Violet ignored the way that smile made her pussy clench and glanced at Max on the couch beside her. The massive Rottweiler gave Grant a cursory look then went back to sleep. Bill was probably asleep on the bed.

"I think everyone's in chill mode."

"I'm seeing that, Miss Ryan."

She watched as he crossed the room. He was

too gorgeous. Tall and blond with a thick gold and red beard, and muscles and muscles for days. Oh and the tattoos. Violet ignored the skip her heart beat tried to pull and set down her tablet. She wasn't too cranky to tilt up her head when he leaned down to kiss her.

"How are you feeling?" he asked when their lips parted. Another shiver to ignore as he stroked her hair.

"Okay. Just a little achy. I feel like my ass is spreading out mostly."

"You're not gonna get any complaints from me in that department." Violet had lost around thirty pounds since they met. She had a lot more to go, but Grant always made it clear that her loved her body in whatever state it was in. Even if she had a bum leg.

He kissed her again before going back to the kitchen. "I got my mom's Christmas cookie recipe so I'm baking today, sister. And I got few other surprises for you too."

"Oh yeah? You fix that time machine so I can go back and unbreak this ankle?"

"Not even close, but I think you'll like it. You want your one of your surprises now?"

Violet shrugged. "Sure."

"Okay. I'll be right back." He grabbed one of

the bigger bags off the floor and walked toward the bedroom, singing along with the Stevie Wonder song that was playing through speakers. That made Violet smile. He had a voice like an angel.

She tried to get back into her e-book, but now that Grant was home she was too restless to focus. She stood and hobbled to the kitchen and started putting away the groceries. She was almost finished when the sound of Grant stomping back into the room forced her to look up.

"HO HO HO! How do I look?"

Her boyfriend was standing there in a full Santa costume complete with a fake beard and a huge bulk of padding around his middle. Violet almost choked. "Um, you look festive. And oddly sexy. Am I supposed to be attracted to Santa?"

"I don't see why not. He's a big, strapping man. Cares about kids, knows how to direct an army of elves. A lot of women find that type of power attractive."

Violet held on to the counter as she looked him up and down. He'd included Santa's signature white gloves. "So is this for me or…?"

"It's for you. You said you missed your window to get your picture taken at the mall with Santa."

"Yeah, I'm not battling a sea of kids and stressed out parents in this cast."

"So take pictures with your own private Santa." Grant came toward her, slipping a large hand under the hem of her shirt. It was a challenge to keep her eyes open. "And I thought we could do a little role playing. You can tell Santa how nice and how naughty you've been, and Santa can dole out presents or punishments accordingly."

Violet was definitely wet now. They hadn't had sex since he's gotten back from Florida. She was still shaken up from her tumble and he was just worried about her getting better. Sex hadn't come up, until now.

"What do you say?"

"Yes."

"Tell me your safe words."

Violet *did* close her eyes then as a shiver rippled over her body. She had no clue how Grant did it, slipped so easily from being this sweet, silly doof of a guy to being one of the sexiest, commanding men she'd ever met, but every time all it took was a simple change in his voice, a look, a touch or a few simple words and she was right there with him, ready to go and more than willing to submit.

She looked back up into his deep blue eyes.

"Yellow if I need you to pull back and Red if I need you to stop."

"Good girl. Now, why don't you step into Santa's workshop."

Violet shrieked as Grant scooped her up and carried her over to his oversized rocking chair beside the couch. At first Violet thought it was a weird thing for a single man to have in his living room, but the piece of furniture had worked its way into a lot of their games. It might get a lot of use in other ways, down the road.

When they were situated Grant pulled out his phone and started snapping pictures of the two of them. Some were intentionally sweet. He pulled down the beard for a few so you could actually see his face and then they took a couple silly shots. Violet stuck her finger up his nose in one and her tongue in his mouth for another. Her favorites ended up being of the one of them sharing a simple kiss and the one where Grant is licking her face.

"So tell me, Violet. What do you want for Christmas?"

Violet let out a light sigh even though her mind was racing. *I want to stop being a scared ass and just tell you. I want you to be happy. I want you to tell me you want this because I think I do. I want you tell me it's going to be okay, that I'm not ruining my career. That this will work.*

"I think I just want you, Santa."

"You think?"

"I know."

"You should show me."

"Switch seats with me, please."

"Not a problem." Grant stood and gently deposited Violet into the rocking chair. She went right for the large belt. Grant caught on and tossed the pillow he had against his stomach then started unbuttoning the jacket, revealing his tight abs under his tank top.

Violet pulled his huge cock out of his boxers and went right to sucking it. She loved the taste of him, the feel of him in her mouth and between her fingers. He rocked his hips in time with the bobbing of her head, stroking her hair and murmuring nasty, sweet nothings until his came down her throat.

"Was that good enough for Santa?" she asked between final licks over the head of his cock.

"Oh yeah." Grant squeezed his eyes shut, something he always did after he came, but wasn't done playing with her yet. Proof was the intense look on his face when he started pulling off the white gloves. He dropped to his knees and slowly started working Violet's pajama pants and underwear down her thighs. He was careful pulling both over her cast and more careful as he spread her legs apart. He slid his fingers into her waiting cunt making Violet whimper. He used his other hand to grip the back of her head.

"I want you to come for me."

"Yes. Oh god, I will."

Grant did that thing he did, read her perfectly, did exactly the right thing. Sometimes she needed it soft and sweet and a little slow, but not today. She wanted it rough. He stood up straighter, pressing their foreheads together as he delivered the finger fucking of a lifetime. Violet couldn't stop thinking about how good it felt, how badly she was wanted to come. How much she loved him. She just blurted it out.

"Oh god! Fuck. Grant, I'm pregnant!"

Grant froze, then yanked his fingers back. Violet let out a laugh that sounded a little manic. "You weren't hurting me."

"Are—are you sure? I—I" He smoothed his hands over her thighs, checking to make sure he hadn't broken anything on her suddenly delicate body.

"Yes, I'm sure and yes, I am pregnant."

"How? I mean—" Grant sat back on his knees and shook his head. "When?"

"I'm about seven weeks."

"That night of the Halloween party."

Violet smiled, nodding. "Yeah." She'd been on the pill and they used condoms frequently, but not always. And it only took one time, that one percent of ineffectiveness. They'd gone to a costume party at the bondage club Grant belonged to and fucked until sun up in one of the private rooms. Condom free.

"Is this okay?" Violet had already made up her mind. They had passing conversations about kids and family, but they hadn't discussed marriage or kids of their own. Still, Grant looked surprised at her question.

"Yes! Of course it's okay."

And now Violet was crying, happy tears though. Grant kissed her, wiping her face. "I would have asked you to marry me months ago if I thought you would say yes."

He had a point. Violet had a feeling that Grant had made up his mind about her, that he wanted to be with her forever. She wanted that too, but she wanted to spend more time just being with him. They could take things slowly, move in together first. After a year or two, talk about getting engaged and she wanted to give her career more time before she thought about kids, but none of that had happened and now there was another human being on the way.

"How do you feel about it?" he asked.

Her hand went to her stomach. She'd been doing that a lot lately. "Good. Scared shitless, but good. There's a lot I'm unpacking about being adopted and having my own kid, but I want her or him. And you."

"Can I be a little selfish and say this is the best Christmas present you could have ever given me?"

"You're never selfish." And that was the truth.

"Or maybe all my selfishness just involves loving you." Grant kissed her one more time, a kissed that morphed into more, a declaration or a pact and then proof that Violet desperately still wanted to come. She took his hand and guided back it between her legs.

"I'll be gentle," he whispered against her lips.

"You don't have to." Violet gripped his wrist and rocked a little closer. "I need you."

Grant looked her in the eye and she knew he meant it when he said "I need you too."

THE END

ABOUT THE AUTHOR

Rebekah was raised in Southern New Hampshire and now lives in Southern California with a great human, one cat whom she loves dearly and another cat she wants to take back to the shelter.

Her interests include Wonder Woman collectibles, cookies, James Taylor, whatever Nicki Minaj is doing at any given time, quality hip-hop, football, American muscle cars, large breed dogs, and the ocean. When she's not working, writing, reading, or sleeping, she is watching HGTV and cartoons or taking dance classes. If given the chance, she will cheat at UNO.

You can find more stories by Rebekah at rebekahweatherspoon.com

You can also chat with Rebekah on Facebook, Twitter, or Tumblr.